SECRETS OF THE WORLD'S WORST MATCHMAKER

PIPER RAYNE

Cover Design: By Hang Le

1st Line Editor: Joy Editing

2nd Line Editor: My Brother's Editor

Proofreader: Shawna Gavas, Behind The Writer

ABOUT SECRETS OF THE WORLD'S WORST MATCHMAKER

Imagine you're a matchmaker and you realize too late you're in love with your childhood best friend. You only have yourself to blame—you're the one who matched him and now he's engaged to be married. When you find yourself in this position there's a few secrets you're going to need to keep...

Secret #1 – Smile when he tells you the happy news, even if your heart cracks in half.

Secret #2 – Don't compare yourself to his beautiful French fiancée. You're just as beautiful.

Secret #3 – Don't tag along to the tux fitting with him alone. Just no.

Secret #4 – Don't help him learn to dance to his wedding song.

Secret #5 – Erase all memories of the two of you through the years when lines blurred for even the briefest of moments.

And the one you never saw coming...

Secret #6 – Definitely, don't stand and object—someone else might just do it for you.

Secrets
of the
World's Worst Matchmaker

The Baileys

Austin Bailey - 36 years old
(Biology Teacher/Baseball Coach)
Savannah Bailey - 34 years old
(Runs Bailey Timber Corp)
Brooklyn Bailey - 31 years old
(Runs Essential Oil Company)
Rome Bailey -29 years old
(Chef)
Denver Bailey - 29 years old
(Bush Pilot)
Juno Bailey - 28 years old
(Matchmaker)
Kingston Bailey - 27 years old
(Smokejumper)
Phoenix Bailey - 23 years old
(Singer)
Sedona Bailey - 23 years old
(Travel Writer)

ONE

Juno

I'm at the bar, waiting for my strawberry lemonade with vodka, when the guests at the Bailey baby shower start yelling about cars and hospitals and kids.

I look over my shoulder and Colton's weaving through chairs and tables with a concerned expression. I roll my eyes and turn back around. Thankfully, before Colton reaches me, the bartender hands over my drink. I'm only three sips in before Colton snatches it out of my grasp and tosses the plastic cup in the trash.

"Hey, I paid for that," I say.

"It's open bar. Savannah just went into labor."

"Good to know." His hand grips my upper arm and I attempt to wrench it back with no success. "Shouldn't you be with your fiancée?" My tone holds more of a sneer to it than usual.

"She had to go into the office. Mr. Beecher's dog is in labor."

I narrow my eyes. "You're more qualified than her."

He huffs and leads me out of Denver and Cleo's airplane hangar, where the triple baby shower is being held because my two sisters and sister-in-law all got pregnant at the same time. And my brother Denver is now engaged, so I have another soon-to-be sister-in-law. Harley, my other sister-in-law, is now pregnant for her fourth time.

"I have a lot of sisters-in-law," I say. "They can handle it."

Colton looks at me. "You've had more than I thought. I have no idea why you hang around that Trey Galger." He shakes his head and scowls. Colton rarely scowls.

My heels push into the gravel, my balance wobbly for a minute before I can really anchor down. "Don't scowl. You smile. That's why all the ladies love you." I pat his cheek.

His scowl turns into a smile, but his grip on my arm loosens at the same time.

I feel myself pitch over, my mind spinning. "Oh God, I'm going to be sick."

Colton has seen me through a lot, and unfortunately, he's held my hair back so many times that he's like the MacGyver of keeping me from getting puke in my hair.

"Hold on." He moves us off the path.

When I see green, all the acid from the lemonade erupts up my throat and I throw up all over a bush.

"You should thank your buddy Trey for all the vodka he fed you today," he says, his fist holding back my hair.

"Please, just take me home," I mumble.

MY CHEEK SLIDES and grinds against the glass from the window being raised and lowered. I blink a few times and glance around. Colton's truck is parked at the curb on Spring Street.

It was touch and go there for a while—I had my head out the window like a panting dog.

"You could have just nudged me awake," I grumble.

Colton chuckles. "What fun would that be?"

I sigh. I don't have the energy to roll my eyes.

"Don't breathe in my direction. Your breath is noxious." He waves his hand in front of his face, laughs at his own damn joke, and leaves me alone in his truck. I sit in solitude for ten seconds before he springs my door open. "Let's go, you're home."

I step down onto the running board and grab a hold of the stability bar to climb out. "Stop holding me back," I tell Colton, swatting my arms in the air.

"Jesus, Juno, your seat belt is on."

I look down and see that he's right. "Anyone can make that mistake."

He bends down into the cab of the truck, his neck dangerously close to my lips. I inhale the scent of his soap and a smell that is just Colton. He's never been big on cologne except that short phase of junior high when he discovered girls. Unfortunately, the smell of men's Polo cologne will remind me of my first kiss forever.

"Did you just sniff me?" he asks, unclicking the seat belt and releasing the pressure on my chest.

"No." I shake my head, dodging eye contact. "Come on, Colton, unless you want me to puke in your truck."

He moves out of my space and I step out. My heel catches something on the sidewalk and my face meets the concrete.

"Oh, you are in rare form tonight." Colton swoops me

up into his arms as though I'm his bride, but I'm not. He has a bride now. Or a bride-to-be at least.

"I always knew you'd make a good husband," I say, touching his stubbly five o'clock shadow. He leaves the house clean-shaven and returns hours later with scruff most guys try for nowadays. That's just one of the many things I know about my best friend.

He props me up higher in his arms. "Juno, get your keys out of your purse."

I open my purse, a little disappointed that he rudely disregarded my compliment. "I don't see them." My fingers dig and dig. "Hmm." I turn the purse upside down and the contents fall all over me.

Colton groans. "Seriously, Juno?"

"How else are we going to know if they're in there?" I look on my stomach for anything that didn't fall to the sidewalk and there they are. "Ah ha!" I pick them up as if I found a hundred-dollar bill on the street.

"Now let's see if you can get it into the lock."

I lean in close to him. "Are you challenging me, Colton Stone?"

"If it gets the key in the lock and you out of my arms quicker, then yes."

I frown and turn my attention to the lock. Colton tries to move me when I miss by a millimeter to the right or the left. Eventually the key goes in, I unlock it, and voila, we're in my apartment building.

He walks up the stairs and he sighs at the second door. "Let's hope you can go two for two."

I get the key in the lock on the first try and raise my hands with a smile.

Colton walks into my apartment and immediately disposes of me on the couch. "Sit tight. I'll be right back."

He jogs back down the stairs. I kick off my heels and walk into my bedroom to change.

I have my dress half off when Colton walks in. "I told you to sit tight."

His eyes flare at the sight of my lacy bra. I'm not sure why I wore a nice bra and panty set today, but right now, I'm happy I did. Although over the years, Colton's seen my much less stellar undergarments.

I struggle for another second with my dress, but the zipper won't cooperate.

"Come here." He relents and breaks the distance between us when I continue to get the fabric caught in the zipper.

He's showing little patience for my antics tonight, and I'm about to remind him of all the times I've nursed him back to health. Like that time he decided we should do a bar crawl in Anchorage with his buddy from college. That was a record two-day hangover.

Then his fingers are on my skin and my mind blurs. The softness of his touch and the smell of him so near calms my jittery body. It always does.

It's one of the reasons I swore we'd never cross that line into a romantic relationship. Why I need him to be in my life forever and not for a brief affair that, if it ends badly, I'll lose him. But all of that seems so senseless right now. My jealousy of his fiancée feels like a living, breathing thing inside me. I watch him work the zipper, the fabric releases, and I catch his eyes. He holds our eye contact.

I want him. I want him to promise me I won't die alone. But I don't want his words—I want his body weighing mine down on the bed. The slow roam of his hands along my body. His smoldering eyes says he's thinking the same thing. He wants me too.

I rise on my tiptoes and my dress pools around my ankles. His gaze dips down, and the fire in his eyes suggests I've sparked his interest.

"Juno," he whispers.

I put my finger to his mouth and press my lips to the hollow of his neck. I continue to place light kisses up his neck and across his jaw. His stubble only spurs thoughts of his face between my legs. If only for tonight, I need him.

Abruptly his hands grip my upper arms and he pushes me away. "You know we can't."

As if someone snapped me out of a hypnosis, my eyes pop open.

"Thanks for the ride home," I say and step away from him.

"Juno, let's talk. I mean..." He stops when I turn my back to him and crawl under the covers of my bed.

"I'm sorry. I should've never done that. You can go home to Brigette now." And I do mean my apology, but the embarrassment flooding every cell in my body is controlling me right now. I threw myself at an engaged man. What the hell is wrong with me?

The bed dips by my feet. "I'll stay. Make sure you don't get sick again."

I tighten the covers over me. "Go home."

THE NEXT DAY, with a pounding head and blurry vision, I pick up my phone to find a million voicemails and text messages from my family.

"*Oh my God!*" I scream, and a loud thump sounds outside my bedroom door.

What the hell was that?

I grab my shoes from my closet and slowly open up my bedroom door.

"Fucking hell." Colton is on all fours on the floor, getting up. He's only in his boxers.

"You stayed?" I ask, wincing as my voice causes my brain to vibrate in my skull. My gaze travels the length of his chest, bouncing down his rippled stomach.

"I wasn't going to leave you alone in your condition," he says, grabbing his pants and putting them on.

"I gotta go. They've all had their babies." I leave him in the living room and head back into my room, pulling out a pair of yoga pants and a sweatshirt.

"Don't you think you should shower first?" He looks me over when I step out and grab my purse. "You look like you got run over by a semi."

I narrow my eyes. "Aren't you a sweet-talker. Is this how you got Brigette to marry you?"

He says nothing and his eyes cast down to the floor. I head to the bathroom to brush my teeth. He comes in and grabs the mouthwash from me. We both spit in the sink at the same time, our eyes catching for the briefest of seconds, but it's like releasing the plug in a bathtub full of water. Memories of last night flood my brain.

They're only pieces as I put them back together in chronological order. The drinks. The acid of the lemonade still raw in my throat. He walks out of the bathroom and I try to remember more. His hands on my skin while he helped with my dress. My lips on his skin. *Oh shit.*

I walk out of the bathroom to find him texting on his phone. No doubt to Brigette, explaining why he had to stay at my apartment last night. She probably thinks nothing of it because she feels no threat with me being Colton's best friend. She trusts me. And I betrayed that trust and Colton's last night.

Fuck, Juno, get your shit together.

He pockets his cell phone. "I'll drive you to the hospital."

"I can drive myself." I want to ignore the confusing feelings where he's concerned and being away from him will make it a lot easier.

"They're like my siblings too. I want to see the babies." He opens the door for me.

I file out with zero intention of acting as if I remember last night at all. But at some point, Colton will corner me about it—hopefully after I arm myself with an excellent excuse.

TWO

One Week Later...

Juno

"Sorry, I'm all out," Greta says, her apron smeared with frosting, proof she had a crazy morning. She only bakes what she bakes, and when she's sold out, she's sold out.

Matchmakers trust their guts, so I should've trusted mine this morning when I woke up with a sour pit in my stomach. I should've pulled the covers over my head, rolled myself into a ball, and forgotten anything existed outside of my bedroom for the rest of the day. But a failing business coupled with a fear of failure pushed me out of bed.

Now I stand inside Sweet Suga Things staring into an empty case that should be filled with donuts. And it probably was an hour ago when I should've been here.

"Your brother grabbed a bunch for the high school science club," Greta says.

Austin, I think with a growl. Instead of showing Greta my annoyance, I smile and peruse the glass cases. "That's okay. I'll find something else."

A potential new client is coming in today, and I want to look professional. So I figured some mouthwatering donuts and coffee from Brewed Awakenings might get him to sign on the dotted line.

As I'm looking over her cookie selection, I hear my last name mentioned behind me. Actually, I overhear two people having a conversation about my family. I slyly glimpse over my shoulder to find two old ladies Grandma Dori's age seated at a table.

"Three of them just had babies. One is pregnant with their fourth. She's now a great-grandma six times over," the one says.

"She must be tired," the other one says.

"You know Dori, it's more bragging material," the first continues.

Did they not notice me walk in?

"She acts like they're so perfect. Even up in Fairbanks, I heard the stories about those twin boys. Always up to no good."

"Well." The first one lowers her voice. "I heard they're all pretty much settled now except for three of them. Even that Phoenix lives with some hotshot music producer from LA."

"My daughter was telling me something about her..."

Greta's expectant eyes on me cause me to stop eavesdropping on the women who think my family is their business.

"Two of those and three of those." I randomly point at the case of cookies. "And fill the rest with those."

Greta's eyes follow my finger, then she grabs a box and tissue to get to work.

"What is the big news around here now?" the second woman asks.

"Colton Stone is engaged."

My heart squeezes. Who are these women and why can't they see I'm right here in this small shop?

"Leta Stone's grandson?" the one asks.

"You know she passed, right? Ten years ago now."

That fall day flashes through my mind. The flowers I stared at the entire time so that I didn't have to think about my parents as the pastor preached about what a great person Colton's grandma was and how we should keep her memory alive.

"Oh, I forgot. It's been so long since I've been back," the second woman says.

"He's engaged to some French veterinarian doing her internship with Dr. Murphy."

There goes that fist squeezing my heart again. French, beautiful, intelligent, and has a helluva lot more going for her than me. I'm sure she would've been up in time to get the donuts.

Before I can turn around for a better look at them, the bell above the door rings and Grandma Dori enters the small bakeshop and cafe as though she owns the place. One of the things I love most about her is that she does what she wants, damn the consequences. The woman's been hurt just like us. She's lost her husband and her son, yet she lives for her nine grandchildren.

"Juno!" she says with excitement.

I turn around fully, glancing at the women to my right. Their faces pale like gossiping church women who got caught by the preacher.

"Hi, Grandma," I say.

She hugs me tightly. She's been hugging me tightly ever since Colton announced his engagement six months ago. She, along with all of my family and probably most of this town, thinks I'm heartbroken. Well, I might be, but I have a doctorate in denial and know how to smack on a smile and assure her I'm fine.

"I was going to go see you after I had a morning coffee with my friends." She gestures to the women. "Come say hello." She drags me toward them, but I stop.

"Let me pay Greta first," I say.

She releases me, and I head to the cash register while Grandma Dori goes to the table. I hear all their exchanges of, "it's been too long" and "I missed you."

"Thanks, Greta." I accept the small box from her.

Grandma Dori is busy, and I might be able to sneak out of here. I'd suffer the consequences later, but they might be worth it. Then again, do I want Grandma Dori busting into my meeting with a potential new client? The answer to that would be hell no. So instead of dodging her, I figure a polite hello and goodbye will be sufficient.

"Juno!" Grandma catches me in her peripheral vision like the hawk she is.

"Hi, Grandma."

The first woman looks familiar, but I don't know her name. The second woman looks at me with scrunched-up gray eyebrows.

"This is my dear friend, Nelly, from Fairbanks. She grew up in Lake Starlight but moved away when you... well." Grandma Dori looks to Nelly for confirmation.

"I think you only had a couple grandkids then." They all laugh.

"Yeah, I suppose you have been gone for decades, not

years," the other woman says, putting out her hand. "I'm Willa. We were all high school friends." She twirls her finger between them.

I shake her hand. "I'm Juno Bailey."

"Are you the one who married the tattoo artist?" Nelly asks.

"No, that's Savannah."

She nods. "The one who's married to the New York millionaire?"

Grandma Dori giggles and her chair screeches across the floor, her hand reaching for me before I bolt. "Juno's our matchmaker."

She wouldn't be the proud grandmother with her arm around me if she knew I'm late on my rent this month.

"That's interesting," Nelly says in the same tone I'd expect if my grandma had told her I'm the tarot card reader with the giant neon sign off the highway.

Meanwhile, Willa keeps staring at me with a puzzled expression. "I never would've guessed that you were a Bailey. Dori, where does the red hair come from?"

I suck in a breath without breaking my smile. This question has plagued me my entire life. People blatantly ask if I'm adopted or if I dye my hair or, worst of all, a foster child the Baileys took into their home. Not looking like any of my siblings is an ongoing joke. Thanks to the movie *Cheaper By the Dozen*, I was called FedEx the entire year I was eleven. I still feel a kinship with Mark Baker from that movie. Being the red-haired kid in a huge family royally sucks.

Grandma looks at me with a sweet smile—the one reserved for when she knows someone is poking an open wound. Austin gets it when people talk about baseball. Savannah when they compare her to our dad in regard to running Bailey Timber. There's a list for each one of my siblings.

"She gets it from my daughter-in-law, Beth's side," Grandma Dori says. "They have matchmaking in their blood as well. Right, Juno?"

I smile at my grandma, giving my rehearsed spiel. "There's a long line of matchmakers on my mom's side. My Aunt Etta was kind of famous for matchmaking famous actors and actresses for years. Casting directors would hire her to figure out who had the best chemistry before casting a film."

"That was ages ago. In the nineteen-forties and fifties," Grandma chimes in.

Neither Nelly nor Willa seem like believers in the matchmaking profession though. Just like me, they smile to be polite.

"And who are you married to, dear?" Nelly asks.

Well, thank you, Nelly. Lay me on the table and slice me open, why don't you?

"She's not married yet. But if I look into my crystal ball, I see that her guy is about to walk into her life any time now."

The bell over the door chimes and we all turn as if Grandma's a fortune teller. In walks Colton, my best friend and the man currently starring in my wet dreams. I squeeze my eyes shut for a moment. I do not want to do this with him in front of Grandma Dori.

"Grandma," I say, sighing heavily. She must have caught him in her peripheral hawk vision.

Colton spots us on his walk up to the counter. "Ladies." He dips his head in our direction like a true gentleman.

His dark hair is perfectly styled and he's freshly shaven, his collared shirt tucked in with no tie. At least he's not wearing his white medical jacket with his name embroidered. That's made too many appearances recently in my recurring dreams. He turns to Greta to order, displaying his ass in a pair of snuggly fit khaki pants. I swear even Willa whimpers.

"I should get going." I kiss Grandma on the cheek and turn to the women. "Very nice to meet you both."

They say their goodbyes, although their eyes linger on Colton.

Willa touches my arm. "If you can get me a guy like him, I'll sign up for you to match me."

My smile slips for a second. *Oh Willa, there's a long line of women who want in Colton's pants, and I should warn you, I'm scrappy.*

"You never know who you'll match with," I joke.

"I'll come by later," Grandma says.

Jeez, the whole reason I stayed here to get judged by her friends was to avoid a visit from Grandma.

"I heard Harley wasn't feeling well," I lie.

She nods and her eyes scrunch. "I better check if she needs help with the kids then." She looks at her friends. "That's Rome's wife. Three kids and another on the way. I just love being a great-grandmother. They need me so much."

I giggle and walk toward the door.

"Juno. Hold up," Colton calls out as my hand is on the door to push through.

I wasn't trying to dodge him. I mean, if he really wanted to talk to me, he knows where to find me. My office is literally one block over from his.

"I figured you were in a rush?" My gaze dips to his two coffees. One for him and one for Brigette, the French goddess. I push the door open and he says the words I've dreaded since I made a fool of myself when I got drunk at my sisters' triple baby shower last week.

"I think we should talk," he says.

Of course he does. We're opposites in every way. He likes to talk all his shit out and I'd rather shove it under a rug.

THREE

Colton

I gave Juno a week and still, she's trying to sneak out behind my back.

At least she actually holds the door open for me. I step out holding the coffees and fall in line with her down the sidewalk. I was on my way to the vet clinic when I spotted her inside Sweet Suga Things. It's about time we hash out what happened.

Without saying a word, we reach SparkFinder, Juno's matchmaking business. She positions the box from the bakery under her arm so she can fiddle with her keys. Usually she would've given me the box to somehow Jenga my way into holding two coffees and a box. I guess we're still in that uncomfortable space.

She flicks on the lights in the small office that holds her desk and a few chairs. No one really ever has to wait to see her since it's mostly by appointment only. There's a room in the back for when she does open companion calls, which is when anyone can come in to be matched with a specific bachelor or bachelorette.

Juno only did two years at college in order to explore what she views as her calling, passed down to her by her ancestors. She truly believes she was born with the gift to match people. The gift of knowing who can reach their fiftieth wedding anniversary versus the ones who will never see past one date. All because she has the same hair as her great-aunt Etta. I humored her through the years but finally challenged her once after biology class when we learned about recessive and dominant genes. One of the many things I love about Juno is the way she can block out any rational explanation for something she believes in. She thinks I don't see the true reason she's so hell-bent on claiming the genealogy, but I do.

"I'm sorry," she says to the pink bakery box instead of me, setting it down and opening it up.

"You don't have to be sorry." I sip my coffee.

"You have to be kidding me." Her chin falls to her chest in pure defeat.

She's struggling with all the Bailey family dynamics, so if whatever is in that box will finally allow her to let it all out, I'll call Dr. Murphy and tell him I'll be fifteen minutes late.

But she turns away from the box, snapping the head off a dinosaur cookie with her teeth. "Greta must have thought I was getting the cookies for Harley."

I walk over and peek in the box to find dinosaur, flower, and baby rattle cookies. "Who are they for?"

She rounds her desk, pretending to go through a stack of papers that I know are print-offs of clients' personal data. "A new client."

"Rolling out the red carpet, huh? What about the water and bags of chips or crackers you usually offer?" I attempt a joke, but she doesn't laugh.

"I really want him as a client, so I figured I'd schmooze him so he signs today."

"If he's smart, he will."

At least we can still hold a conversation.

She peeks up and smiles. Her makeup is heavier today, her hair more curled. This client must be important. "I shouldn't have done what I did. I put you in a horrible situation."

I shake my head. "It's fine. Honestly."

She nods. "It was wrong to Brigette. It's just…"

A large part of me wants her to continue. Tell me why she suddenly wanted to kiss me that night, but the other part, the part that knows I can't entertain that option, says it's a good thing the words go unspoken. "It's okay, Juno. I'm not going to tell her anything. We're just getting used to this new situation."

A new situation that I caused.

"Friends?" she asks, smiling at me.

"Always."

Her chest rises and falls with a deep breath, and her gaze darts to the clicking clock that's the only sound in the room.

"Oh, here you go." I set her coffee on her desk. "I better go. Rhys is coming in with his new dog today."

"You don't have to give me Brigette's coffee just because I'm upset." She picks it up and holds it out to me.

How did I not consider this wedge Brigette is putting between us? "I bought the coffee for you."

"Oh." She sips it as if she needs the caffeine to survive. "Thanks."

I nod. "Brigette only drinks from Brewed Awakenings. Says it's the most like back home."

Her small smile falls. "I better get set up for him."

"How about we have lunch? Tomorrow?"

"Sure. Text me. Sorry, I really have to use the bathroom." She sets down her coffee and walks away. "Have a great day."

And the bathroom door shuts.

Usually, I'd bust the bathroom door open and call her out on her bullshit, but since I'm the reason she can't look at me, I leave.

"BONJOUR," Brigette says when I walk through the back door of Four Paws Veterinary Clinic. She's already wearing her white jacket and holds her Brewed Awakenings coffee in hand.

"Good morning."

She sits at the small table in our break room while I go to my locker to put on my white coat.

"You seem down," she says.

I shake my head. She doesn't need me to convey my guilt that my best friend has no idea how to handle the fact I'm getting married. So much so, that she convinced herself a week ago that she wanted me. I've made my feelings clear over the years, but Juno's always had a Heisman trophy arm poised in my direction. I understood her hang-ups about us being a couple, but it didn't make it any easier to take. I've done stupid shit witnessing her with someone else too, so can I really blame her? No.

"I'm fine. Just Monday." I slide my arms through my white jacket and shut my locker.

"Are you sure? You can talk to me about anything."

Brigette knows the situation with Juno, and I could talk to her about it and she'd understand, but I think she might feel bad about it too. And right now, I just want to drown myself in work.

"No, you ready to start the day?" I ask.

She nods, sipping her coffee. I pick up mine and we walk to the receptionist's area. Our vet assistant, Hillary, is prepping the paperwork.

"Good morning, Hillary. Morning, Lori," I say to Hillary and our receptionist, Dr. Murphy's sister, Lori.

"Good morning, you two lovebirds." Hillary winks.

Brigette slides her arm through mine and rises on her toes to kiss my cheek. "I'm afraid my fiancé has a horrible case of the Mondays."

They both laugh because Brigette has been brushing up on her American movies. I made a list of my favorites and she pulls one line out each time she watches one.

"*Office Space*." We look up to see Rhys standing in the small welcome opening. "I believe you have my stapler."

We all laugh. Rhys is a tattoo artist down at Smokin' Guns, which Juno's brother-in-law, Liam Kelly, owns.

"Hey, Rhys." I put my hand on Lori's shoulder. "Sorry, I forgot to tell you that Rhys was coming in this morning. I ran into him this weekend and he adopted a new puppy."

"Okay, I just need you to fill out this paperwork first." Lori slides out of her chair to grab a prepared clipboard. "I would've had the file prepped if I'd known you were coming, so you wouldn't have to fill it out while holding your dog."

Lori's neurotic behavior shines brightly in front of our newest customer. Although if Dr. Murphy ever retires, I'm sure it'll be part of the agreement that I have to keep Lori on.

"I'll watch him." Brigette sips her coffee tosses the cup in the trash can, nudging me out of the way. I've never seen her not finish her entire coffee—except when I took her to Lard Have Mercy once. She lives for the stuff.

"Oh, that would be great." Rhys eyes her from head to toe now that she's on the other side of the window.

Brigette is beautiful. She danced for years until she found her true passion was animals. She came to Alaska on vacation and decided this is where she wanted to go to school, if for nothing more than to experience living in Alaska. She's kind of a bucket-list girl, which scares me because I'm not a bucket list kind of guy. I'm born, bred, and happy to die in Lake Starlight. But she swears she loves it here, so all I can really do is trust her.

"Rhys, this is my fiancée, Brigette," I introduce them, which causes Rhys's gaze to snap back up to Brigette's eyes instead of her breasts.

She does dress in some revealing tops on occasion. Dr. Murphy told me Lori doesn't approve and would like me to talk to Brigette about it now that we're engaged, but I'd rather be hit by a Mack truck than tell a woman another woman disapproves of what she's wearing.

All I hear is Brigette 'cooing' and 'ahhing' over the new dog, Clyde. I peek over the ledge to get a look at the breed and type. Usually I can predict the type of dog someone will buy. The fact that Austin, Juno's older brother, got a husky fits. Austin loves the outdoors and would want a dog who loves it too. Juno's sister, Brooklyn, has Gizmo, who is a cross between husky and corgi. One look at her and her husband, Wyatt, says they're purse-dog people. Nothing too big to ruin their expensive stuff.

I would have expected Rhys to get a Labrador or a golden retriever. A big dog that needs exercise. Not the bulldog that's slobbering all over Brigette's coat at the moment. The name Clyde fits him perfectly, but I'm surprised Rhys would pick such a lazy dog.

Rhys finishes fairly quickly and hands the paperwork to Lori, but instead of letting me take them to go examine the little guy, Lori insists she needs to make up the folder first. So we all wait for her to color code and label it, then type information into the computer. She's organized, don't get me wrong, but she's inflexible.

Finally, she hands the folder to Hillary, her dark eyes on me. "She gets it first."

I raise my hand. "Hillary, let me know when you're done."

I disappear before I say something I'll regret. Something that would cause Dr. Murphy to have a conversation with me. Something that could jeopardize me getting the practice.

"I'll be just a moment." Hillary smiles and opens the door to the waiting room. "Come on in, Clyde."

"I think he's in love," Rhys says.

I glance over my shoulder to see Clyde nestled in Brigette's arms, his face right between her large breasts. I huff a laugh because I'm pretty sure it's not only Clyde who likes what Brigette has to offer.

FOUR

Juno

I'm sitting at my desk, looking through files of the women who came in a few months ago for another bachelor, pulling out the ones I think might be a fit based on the little bit of information I got from my potential new client on the phone.

But I can't focus. My mind keeps wandering to this morning with Colton. A man I've known almost as long as I knew my father. Colton's my rock, the one person I depend on, and his upcoming wedding will change that. He's not going to run over with soup when I'm sick, veg out with me when I'm depressed, call me up when he has something he needs to talk about. We won't go on our road trips on the first real nice day of spring. Or cheer on his alma mater, the Rams, on opening college football day. He'll do all those things with *her*.

The bell on my door dings, pulling me from the funk

I've found myself in since the announcement of his upcoming nuptials. A tall, handsome man with dimples so deep, most women drool over them stands inside my office. I've had beautiful women use my services on occasion because they feel like they keep attracting the same type of man, but drop-dead gorgeous men are unicorns in my office.

"Hi." I push away from my desk, holding out my hand while breaking the distance. "Juno Bailey, your matchmaker."

He shakes my hand and I make a mental note: firm handshake, smooth skin, kind smile. "Hello. I'm Jason Graham."

"Nice to meet you. Please help yourself to a cookie. Sorry about the children's theme going on. Mix up at the bakery. Would you like a drink?"

He glances at the box and shakes his head. A guy like him probably stays away from refined sugar and has already had a protein shake after his workout this morning. *Think, Juno.* "Thanks, but I'm good."

"Have a seat." I motion for him to sit in the chair in front of my desk.

"This place is cute. I don't come to Lake Starlight very often."

I eye the tattoo peeking out of his shirt sleeve. He's dressed casually, in jeans and a nice V-neck T-shirt, but a T-shirt no less. Which means he doesn't have a demanding white-collar job that takes him out of the state. Many women don't prefer when a man has to constantly travel for work.

"Thanks. I'm born and bred, so I'm a bit prejudiced. Go Spartans!" I raise my fist.

"No worries, I'm not originally from Greywall."

That's good, since Greywall and Lake Starlight are

rivals in the high school sports circuit. So much so that sometimes grown adults still have riffs.

"When did you move to Greywall?" I ask.

"About two years ago. I'm originally from Seattle. Followed my fiancée to Alaska."

I frown. "I'm sorry."

He looks at me skeptically.

"I figure if you're coming to a matchmaker, you're no longer engaged?"

He laughs and nods. "Right. Slow on the uptake. Our engagement ended about six months after I followed her here, but I fell in love with Alaska. Go figure, right? I love the one state with more males than females."

I smile. "Don't worry. I can't imagine you're a hard person to match. Mind if we start in on the personal questions?"

He straightens in his chair. "Shoot."

I ask him the series of questions I've developed and find out that he's an optometrist. His office is closed on Mondays, but that means he works Saturdays. He loves the outdoors, which is a given since he fell in love with Alaska. You have to be somewhat of an outdoors person to live here. He's an avid hiker and adventure enthusiast.

"Have you ever done an excursion with Lifetime Adventures?" I ask.

"No. When I first moved here, I checked them out, they seemed really serious and I felt like I might not be able to keep up, but I see they have some novice survivalist excursions now."

"My brother owns it." I pull one of their cards out of my desk. "Tell him I sent you."

He twirls it in his hand. "Perfect."

"Now let's get into what you're looking for in a woman.

Please feel free to be as picky and specific as you'd like. I can't say I'll get all the boxes checked—I might find a blonde who's better suited for you than a brunette—but tell me what you're attracted to."

He eyes me and his cheeks turn a slight pink. "Are you really asking me to pick my dream girl?"

"I am."

He rubs his hands together, and we both laugh. "I'd say she's five-five or so. A smile that makes you feel like you walked into a house that smells of freshly baked bread. Eyes that show all her feelings."

My pen stops on the paper. "That's it?"

He laughs. "She has to want a serious relationship and have a sense of humor. I know a lot of guys probably come in here and tell you that. But for me, it's a must. To be honest, there's a reason I came to you."

I drop the pen on the paper. "Why?"

"I know of your family. I hope that doesn't sound creepy." He cringes.

It should, but it doesn't. The Baileys are pretty well known in the area. Mostly because when your parents die at the same time and leave their nine kids as orphans, a small town bands together and I think, in a sense, a lot of Lake Starlight's residents think of us as their own.

"I came here for the last Founder's Day with a friend and he was telling me the story of your family during the parade. The Baileys are fortunate at finding love, so I figured I'd go to the expert."

I inwardly laugh. He wouldn't think that if he knew I'm about to watch my best friend marry someone else because after years of friendship, I just realized I love him. I wouldn't call me an expert in anything other than failure.

"Well, my siblings have had success, but I must warn you, I'm still single, along with two other siblings."

He chuckles. "I find that hard to believe."

"Well, Kingston is messed up—that's a whole other story—and Sedona is still young. She's pretty serious about this soccer—"

"I meant that you're single."

I rear back and heat fills my cheek. *Stop blushing. You cannot blush in front of a client.* "Oh. Yeah. Well."

Pull it together, Juno.

I manage to straighten my back in the chair and stop being awkward as hell just because someone compliments me.

"I can't date a client." Best to be upfront if that's what he's getting at.

"What if I wasn't a client?" He raises his eyebrows. "I guess I expected someone more like her when I walked in." He points at the picture of my Aunt Etta on the wall.

Yeah, he's right, she sure looked the part. She was in her seventies when that picture was taken, red curled hair and a hat, no skin showing except her face.

"That's my Aunt Etta. I get my matchmaking skills from her."

"Really?"

"Yeah, that's what my mom always said. I'm the only Bailey with red hair, and there's a long line of redheads on my mom's side who had the craft of matchmaking at their fingertips."

He nods and I realize I'm dodging his advance.

"So how about a date, Juno?"

Jason isn't the first guy to hit on me, but usually, it's not a potential client—it's the guys I bring in to set up with my bachelorettes. They don't get a call back. But

Jason's not doing this in a sleezy way like those guys did.

"I'm not sure."

Colton comes to my mind. Then Brigette right after.

Her in a white dress and Colton waiting at the end of the aisle. What choice do I have at this point? Move on and maybe put Colton back into the friend box.

"Sure."

He smiles wide. Those dimples could fit quarters. "Great. How about Saturday?"

I glance at my calendar. "Perfect."

He stands and pulls his phone out of his pocket. "Should we exchange numbers?"

"Yeah. I guess so."

We exchange our personal numbers and he shoves his phone into his pocket. "I'll call you with specifics." He holds out his hand. "See how great you are? You already fixed me up." He winks, and I smile.

"Don't give me too much credit."

He steps back and waves to me one more time before walking out the door.

I snap off a piece of a baby rattle cookie. This can be my lunch. I'm brushing the crumbs off my chest when the door dings again.

"Hey, Miss Juno." Earl, the mail carrier, comes in. "Mail call." He drops it on my desk.

"Thank you, Earl. Have a cookie or two," I say.

Earl is a transplant from Alabama. Moved up here to be with his daughter and her husband so he could be near his grandchildren after his wife died.

"Don't mind if I do." He looks at them. "Oh, dinosaur, my favorite." He laughs and nods his thank you. "Have a great day, Miss Juno. See you tomorrow."

He leaves and I walk across the room to pick up my mail and there it is—my electricity bill. I see the red through the envelope, their way of saying, "Open this up and pay, or else." I tear the envelope open and sure enough, there's a shut-off notice.

Great. I managed to get a date and not a client. How do I expect to pay these bills?

I sit down and let my forehead fall to the desk.

The door opens and I quickly right myself, finding Grandma Dori and Colton standing there. She has her arm through his arm, and knowing her, she's holding on tight to make sure he can't escape.

"Juno, you can't just nap at work," she says.

"I wasn't napping." I quickly straighten my papers, shoving the past due notices into the drawer.

When I look up, Colton's watching me intently. I've always told him he should have been a detective. He can scent out when something's off like a drug-sniffing dog.

"People can see you through the window," Grandma continues. "At least lock your door. Maybe we get you one of those separator fan things."

"A room divider," Colton says.

Grandma pats his hand. "That's it. Thank you, Colton." She unhooks her arm from his and detours to the cookies, grabbing a flower one before sitting down in front of me. "Don't let those nosey women this morning bring up those feelings from the past, dear." She bites off part of the cookie and looks at it. "I'm going to snag some of these for Calista, Dion, and Phoebe."

"Go ahead. I'll eat them all if you don't."

"What do you mean about past feelings?" Colton asks, leaning against the table I have in the front with my promotional materials on top.

"It's nothing," I say.

"The fact that she's the only redhead in the Baileys," Grandma kindly fills him in.

"Oh, that," Colton says, crossing his arms, his gaze shifting to the picture of Aunt Etta.

I know exactly what he thinks about matchmaking being passed down to me from my ancestors. It doesn't match up with his scientific beliefs.

He pushes off the table. "I gotta go."

"Where are you going?" I ask, figuring lunch since it's almost noon now.

"Oh, that's why we came in here. I found Colton right as he was leaving the office. You have to go with him. I'll watch the office." She shoos me out of my chair.

I stand, panic like a hot poker in the stomach because of what's in that drawer. Grandma Dori is a snoop and she'll find my bills.

"I can close the office, but where are you going?" I ask Colton because I'm more likely to get the answer from him.

His face looks pained as if the last thing he wants to do is tell me. Just like when he told me he was engaged. "I have to pick out a tux."

"And he needs a woman's touch." I move to sit back down in my chair, but I sit in Grandma Dori's lap. "Oh dear, you're much too heavy to sit on my lap nowadays." She laughs.

I cannot go tux shopping with him. "Surely you have better style than I do," I say to Grandma.

"Well, that's a given, but I'm sure Colton's not up for my hand up his crotch to make sure his inseam is right."

"I think the tailor will be doing that." Colton tilts his head and gives me a look that says, "You better come, I am not going with your grandma."

But I know if I see him in a tux, I might blurt out my true feelings, which will only make things worse.

Grandma's already opening the right desk drawer and searching its contents.

I move to the table and package up the cookies. "You need to go check on Harley. She called again earlier and said she was really suffering from morning sickness." I cringe.

Her lipsticked mouth turns into an O and she springs up as if she's twenty years younger and snags the box out of my hands. "See you two later."

"Well?" Colton asks after she's left.

"What?" I ask, pretending to straighten my pamphlets on the table.

"Tell me what to buy like you did for senior prom?" He raises his eyebrows.

He's been there for me my entire life. From the minute my world crashed around me until now. He helped me pick up pieces when I had no desire to do it. How can I say no to him?

I can't.

"Let me grab my purse."

FIVE

Juno

Thirteen years old

My parents are away on one of my mom's business trips. It's a return trip to Juneau to talk about the changes since she'd written about the city back when I was conceived. As gross as it is, each of my siblings are named after the city we were conceived in. Thankfully, my parents decided to spell my name differently.

Brooklyn has been in charge of us—with plenty of drop-ins from Grandma Dori—but she's dating Trent Gebhart and asked Grandma if she can go out on a date with him to the movies tonight. Since Grandma has card night with her friends, she's taking Phoenix, Sedona, and Kingston to her place for a sleepover, which means Rome, Denver, and I are on our own.

"Now remember, no parties," Grandma scolds us with

her finger pointed where we all stand on the driveway, saying our goodbyes. "You know I'll have the sheriff checking every hour."

She's talking more to Rome and Denver than me.

"Oh, G'Ma D, you know we won't do that. We're just gonna chill at home." Denver puts his arm around her shoulders.

"I'm gonna make us some pizza." Rome wraps his arm around my shoulders and winks at me.

That's not a good sign.

"You're not too old for me to put you over my knee," Grandma warns.

Phoenix screams at the top of her lungs, interrupting Grandma's lecture.

Grandma whips open the back door of her Cadillac. "What on Earth?"

"Kingston is touching me," Phoenix says.

"So what?"

"So he's sweaty from playing basketball."

Grandma Dori sighs. "Get in the front seat, Kingston."

"What? Why can't I sit in the front?" Phoenix yells. "Why does he get to?"

"He's older," Grandma says and slams the door shut. "This is a test, boys. I'm trusting you."

The twins smile and wave goodbye like little church usher boys until she's out of the driveway.

Then Rome turns to me. "You cool if we leave you alone for, like, two hours?"

"What? Why?"

"There's a fight going down between Liam and Jack Billings." Denver's already on his bike.

"Just call Colton or Emily and ask them to come over," Rome says, hopping on his bike.

They ride off down the driveway. Fifteen minutes later, Colton's riding his bike up to my house. His parents only live two doors down, which is still a mile away, but to us, it's close enough.

"Hey," I say.

"You're really alone?" he asks, walking up the front steps of my house. He's wearing jean shorts and his faded Colorado State T-shirt.

"Yep. Emily's coming over too."

"Cool." He walks into my house and I shut the door. "What are we gonna do?"

I shrug. "I guess what we always do. Want to play pool or something?"

"After we raid the fridge," he says, beelining it to my kitchen.

He's always hungry now. He emerges from the kitchen with two cans of pop and a bag of Cheetos and heads toward the basement door.

I start to follow, but the bell rings. "I'll meet you down there."

I open my front door and Emily is standing on my porch with Xavier.

"Xavier was over at my place." Emily walks in.

"What's up, Bailey?" Xavier asks, nodding.

I roll my eyes because I hate Xavier. The fact he calls me by my last name as if it's an insult annoys me.

"Colton's already downstairs," I tell them.

"Xavier, go on down," Emily says. "I have to talk to Juno for a second."

Xavier walks down the hallway to my basement stairs, and Emily tugs me by my sweatshirt sleeve into the kitchen.

"What?" I say, pulling my arm back.

"Xavier kissed me," she says. "We were on my back

porch, chilling and listening to music, and then he just kissed me."

My mouth drops open. "Tongue?"

"A little."

"A little?" My body shivers because I would never want Xavier's tongue in my mouth.

"The tip." I stare at her and she laughs. "It sounds worse than it is." She twirls her blonde hair around her finger.

"What did you do?"

She laughs. "I kissed him back."

"But how?"

A lot of kids at school are kissing. Or at least they're saying they're kissing. There're all kinds of games people are playing, like Spin the Bottle and Seven Minutes in Heaven. This is a monumental moment for Emily—her first kiss is all she's been talking about—but the fact that it's with Xavier—whose name is always mentioned in the kissing stories—makes me think it might not be as special to him as it is to Emily. Then again, I'm not sure she cared who she kissed as long as she can say she did.

She jumps off the counter and grabs an empty olive oil bottle from the counter that's there to be recycled. "And now it's your turn. We're playing Spin the Bottle."

"I'm not kissing Xavier." I snatch the bottle and put it back where she found it.

"Of course you're not. You're kissing Colton."

My eyes widen. "Ew. I think that kiss starved your brain of oxygen."

"Come on." She hits me with her shoulder and grabs the bottle back.

I reach for it, but she holds it up higher than I can reach. "I'm not kissing Colton."

"Why?" She juts out her hip.

"Because he's my best friend."

Her eyes narrow. "I thought I was your best friend."

"You're both my best friends. Now give me the bottle."

"Okay, but I am your best friend. Everyone knows once you reach a certain age, guys and girls can't just be friends." She raises the bottle in the air. Damn me being height-challenged. "At least you can trust Colton not to make fun of you if you kiss bad."

"Who says I'll be bad?" She doesn't know. I've practiced on my hand before, and with so many older siblings, I've seen way more R-rated movies than her.

"No one, but remember Olivia Reeder last year? How that jerk, Ian, told everyone she was like kissing a bottle and had no idea what she was doing?"

I fall back down to my heels. She's right. Olivia missed a week of school until her parents forced her to go back. Ian and his friends still pick on her when they finish their Snapple bottles, sticking their tongues inside and pretending to make out with them.

"Colton's the safe bet," Emily says.

"What if it changes things?"

She tugs the arm of my sweatshirt. "It's Colton. Please. A kiss can be just a kiss. You overthink everything."

She practically pulls me down the stairs, and when we reach the bottom, Colton looks up as he positions his shot on the table. Xavier eyes the bottle in Emily's hand.

"Guess what we're going to play now?" She holds up the bottle.

Xavier ditches his pool cue on the table. Colton stands up straight and looks at me.

"Spin the Bottle." Xavier meets Emily, who's already sitting on the floor in front of the couches.

"Why?" Colton asks.

"What kind of guy are you? Get your butt over here." Emily pats the spot next to her.

But Colton continues to look at me, questions filling his eyes. He's not like Xavier and the other boys. He's never been rumored to have kissed anyone, but then again, he's usually with me on the weekends.

I shrug and sit down. This is the best thing for both of us, even if he doesn't know it yet. How great would it be if both of our first kisses are with each other? If one of us messes up, we'd never tell anyone else.

"We need music." Xavier stands and fiddles with our stereo until the Black Eyed Peas play, which means Brooklyn was listening to it last. He sits back down between Emily and me.

Colton fiddles with the shoelaces of his Converse, looking at me out the corner of his eye.

"Okay, remember if it lands on the same couple three times, that means tongue action. Juno's house, so she goes first." Emily eyes Xavier and they share a laugh. They're all about this game.

I twirl the bottle with my hand and swallow, watching the bottle spin and spin, releasing my breath when it bypasses Xavier. At this point, I'd rather kiss Emily than Xavier. It slows between Emily and Colton. We look at them for the answer since this is their game.

"Midway always goes to the right. You and Colton," Emily says.

We look at each other and I press my hands on the floor to lean forward. He does the same and our lips meet, pressing together for the briefest moment. Then I'm back in my space as quickly as possible. That wasn't so bad. Colton continues to play with his shoelace and all I can feel is how red my cheeks are.

Xavier and Emily stare at us as if we're about to rate the kiss. When neither of us says anything, Xavier spins the bottle and it lands on Colton, to which Xavier says redo. Then it spins and points at Emily. They kiss with tongue on the first go. I guess once you go tongue, you don't go back. Emily spins, and it lands on Colton. I watch as he kisses her just like he did me, glancing in my direction. Colton spins, and my heart is in my throat as it stops between Xavier and me.

"That's you, Juno," Emily says.

"But you said—"

"I'm not kissing him," Xavier says.

"Come on, Juno. It's only the second time," Colton says.

I lean forward and our lips stay connected a little longer than the first time, and I realize how soft his lips are. He got his braces off last year and he's been obsessed with Chapstick since. I vow to never make fun of his addiction again.

Emily wiggles in her spot, almost clapping and giddy as if she had the kiss.

I spin the bottle and it lands on Xavier. He gets the quickest peck ever from me and I run my hand over my lips after. Emily's spin lands back on Colton, and I watch them kiss again.

As Colton's hand covers the bottle, my gut twists, and I have no idea if it's because if it lands on me, we have to use tongue, or if it's the fact that if it lands on Emily, his first tongue kiss will be with her.

My eyes follow the bottle's movement, and I realize as it slows down that I'm holding my breath. It comes to a stop right between Colton and me, and a rush of hot air flows out of my mouth.

The room seems so small, as if there's a spotlight above

us as our eyes lock, both of us conveying that this is it. We're going to have our first kiss in front of our friends.

We lean in toward each other and our lips touch.

"You have to use tongue," Emily says.

Colton presses a little firmer, his tongue sliding between the seam of my lips. I open for him, not sure what exactly I'm supposed to do. All I can think about is that Colton is kissing me, his tongue is in my mouth, and a funny feeling rushes to the pit of my stomach. I kind of like kissing Colton. I mean, it's not horrible.

Then the lights flicker on and footsteps barrel down the stairs. "What's going on here?" Brooklyn says.

Colton and I fly apart, and I wipe my mouth.

"Your friends have to leave," she says, turning off the radio. Her eyes are red and swollen. "Where are Rome and Denver?"

"Why do they have to leave?" I stand up and press the stereo back on.

A minute later, more footsteps sound on the stairs.

"Brooklyn!" Grandma Dori yells downstairs. "I'm calling Austin and then Savannah."

Brooklyn presses the stereo off. "I told you, Juno, your friends need to go." A tear slips from her eye.

"Where are the boys?" Grandma asks from upstairs.

"What's going on?" I ask.

"Just have your friends go home. Grandma needs to speak to all the kids." Brooklyn heads up the stairs, wiping at her face the entire time.

"Did something happen?" Colton asks at my side.

"I'm not sure, but I guess you guys should go."

My friends leave, and I sit on the floor of our family room with my siblings, minus Austin and Savannah, who are away at college.

Grandma sits on a chair and fists her shaking hands. For the first time ever she's having a hard time talking. "There's been an accident."

Brooklyn breaks down in sobs. Kingston looks at her as though he doesn't understand, and Phoenix and Sedona start crying.

"Your mom and dad are in the hospital up in Juneau," Grandma says.

My heart plummets into my stomach.

Ten minutes later is when my grandma says it's serious, that my parents are really hurt but the doctors are trying to fix them up. She says we should think positive, but the fact that she's called Austin and Savannah home is a bad sign.

I walk out our front door because my dad always said no matter where they are, we all share the same sky—and almost scream when I see Colton on the steps of my house.

He stands. "It seemed serious. I stayed in case you needed me."

We sit on the steps of my house, our legs brushing, but we don't talk about the kiss we shared. He doesn't hug me or tell me it will be okay; he just sits there.

It's then that I know Colton will be a fixture in my life forever, not just here temporarily like Emily said. A friendship like ours can stand the test of time.

SIX

Colton

I open the door of the only tuxedo shop in town and let Juno walk through first.

Mr. Johnson smiles at us and comes around from behind the counter. "Juno Bailey. I didn't think I'd get to see your beautiful face today."

He opens his arms and Juno falls right in, hugging him back. Mr. Johnson was a friend of our dads. If you grew up in Lake Starlight, you knew one another. So just like my dad, every guy who went to school with Mr. Bailey feels a sense of responsibility to the Bailey kids.

"Hi, Mr. Johnson. I'm here to tell this guy what to wear for the big day." She thumbs toward me.

"He definitely needs the help." Mr. Johnson smiles at me over Juno's shoulder.

"Whatever. Let's see what you got for me." I rub my hands together.

Juno sits in one of the big leather chairs by the fitting room. "Fashion show time." She pulls out her phone. "I'll take a picture of each so we can see if it's camera-worthy."

"I already set some things in dressing room number one." Mr. Johnson points at the small hallway. "I figured you for more of a classic guy, but I didn't know how dressy you wanted to get. Don't worry about fit. I'll tailor it."

"Yeah. Thanks."

"I want to see each one, Stone." Juno crosses her legs and picks up a magazine from the small round table. She's back to her usual self, which hopefully means we've moved past the awkwardness of last weekend.

"Yeah, yeah."

I shut the door of the fitting room and overhear Mr. Johnson asking Juno about her siblings, how the new babies are and how the new mothers are holding up. She's polite and cheerful, but unfortunately, I hear the tone in her voice that says she's being overly polite. Not that she's not happy for her siblings—Juno lives for her family—but something is really bothering her lately. It's like she's in a rush to find someone one day, and the next she thinks she's destined to be the solo Bailey.

I slide my slacks off my body and fold them neatly on the bench, then exchange my button-down for the classic white shirt Mr. Johnson put in the room. As I'm buttoning it, all I can think about is how I always saw Juno as my bride. How it wouldn't be her voice on the other side of the fitting room door because she wouldn't want to see me before our wedding day. But here I am marrying Brigette instead. It's all so different than what I imagined.

I tuck the white shirt into the classic gray slacks, adjusting the waist to fit better.

I've always been a commitment guy. Always ready for

the next step. I'm not surprised to be getting married, but I am surprised to whom, since I promised my heart to someone other than my bride-to-be a long time ago. I witnessed my parents' loving marriage all my life. I saw how much they leaned on one another when my grandparents passed away and when Tim and Beth Bailey died. When fishing season wasn't going well, and my mom had to get a job. Even though my dad was depressed because he felt it was a man's place to bring money into the household, he made sure that all the household tasks were done. That there was a hot meal for my mom when she came home, and the laundry was all put away. They saw one another through thick and thin, and I want the same. A partner in life.

My arms glide through the black jacket and I straighten the white shirt underneath by pulling on the cuffs. I look goofy as hell.

"Come on, Stone, we're waiting," Juno yells.

I walk out in the tuxedo to the three mirrors and step up on the box.

Juno says nothing. She looks me up and down, but no words leave her mouth.

"Well? I look ridiculous, right?"

"You look grown-up." Her lip trembles for a millisecond before she swallows and masks any emotion. "Where's the lanky kid who broke his arm trying to be cool on a skateboard?" She lets out a strained laugh and stands, taking a picture with her phone.

"Where's the girl with bubble gum all over her face because she shoved so many pieces of Hubba Bubba in there to blow the *Guinness Book of World Records'* biggest bubble?"

She smiles. We could go on and on about all our memories. The good ones. The funny ones. We never talk about the serious ones. Juno likes to keep those in a locked vault. Unfortunately, many of those times are memories I like to relive. Not because they're bad, but because of what happened when we comforted one another. The lingering touches, the tight hugs and long holds. The short kisses to cheeks that would continue down the other's face until our lips met. The soft, hesitant kisses to test if the other one was on the same page. Times when the line would blur slightly with the excuse of comfort.

"Circle around now." She twirls her finger in the air.

I do as she says, acting like a runway model with my hands tucked into the pockets of my pants.

"You are a classic kind of guy, aren't you?" Her eyes peruse me and my blood whooshes through my body at her attention.

"I think it's too dressy though. I mean, we're having a garden wedding at Selene's."

She stares at me, her finger to her lips, tapping like she's a judge on *Top Model*. "Let's see what else Mr. Johnson found."

I disappear down the hallway and hear her laugh at something Mr. Johnson says.

I take off the tux—which is the one I wore in my head while I waited for Juno to walk down the aisle toward me—and put on a navy suit with a white shirt and burgundy tie. This works better for my wedding with Brigette.

MR. JOHNSON TAKES all my measurements, and I put down the deposit on the suit.

"Lunch?" I ask Juno after we're out of the shop.

"I should probably get back to the office."

"That client already come in today?"

"Yeah." Her mouth opens as though she's going to say something else, but she doesn't.

"Then we're going to lunch. A quick one at Lard Have Mercy." I bend down so we're eye to eye.

She nods, and we both turn to take the shortcut through the gazebo and park over to Main Street. Neither of us talks much on the way to the small diner.

We're seated in a booth in the far corner, with a view of the park. We've eaten here so many times I've lost count. At thirteen, we came here for fries and milkshakes. By high school, I was getting burgers and onion rings while Juno ordered grilled cheese and ate half my rings. She always refused to order her own. When I came home from college, I started ordering the Salisbury steak while Juno shifted to salads.

"I'll have soup and salad," she tells the waitress.

"I'll have a cheeseburger and onion rings."

Juno's head snaps up from the menu. "No chicken and dumplings, old man?"

We hand our menus to the waitress. "I'm feeling nostalgic."

She tilts her head. "Why?"

I shrug. "I have no idea, but I bet you'll steal a few onion rings."

"I like my soup and salad, thank you," she says. "Not to mention I have to fit into my dress for your wedding."

"Oh yeah, Brigette mentioned that we haven't gotten your RSVP yet."

She takes the bin of jams, organizing them so all the same flavors are once again back together. "Oh, sorry. I thought I had."

"Are you bringing anyone?" I ask the question that's been burning inside me.

Brigette actually didn't notice we didn't get her RSVP. I did—because I want to know if she's bringing that douchebag Trey from Los Angeles.

She shakes her head. "No."

"What's going on with Trey?"

She's been tight-lipped about him since whatever happened between them last year, but I know *something* happened. The jokes her sisters make that quickly cut off when they remember I'm in the room are a pretty good indicator. Trey Galger is a record label owner who's friends with Phoenix's boyfriend. He flies his private jet into town every now and then. I hate the guy on principle that he's not what Juno needs in her life.

She gives me that confused look she does every time I ask about him. "Nothing is going on. The baby shower was the first time I'd seen him in, like, six months."

For some reason, her brushing it off stokes enough anger inside that I blurt out what I'm really feeling. "Juno, I can't do this anymore."

Her head rears back. "What are you talking about?"

"I'm talking about this awkwardness between us. I get that I conveyed to you that I didn't like Trey and I know I'm getting married and then the whole kiss thing last weekend, but I told you not to worry about it. We're best friends. What's happening to us?"

The waitress comes over and brings us our drinks.

We nod our thanks and Juno waits until she leaves to respond. "I'm just embarrassed."

"Why? It's not like we haven't done things like that before."

"Colton!" She looks around and leans forward, lowering

her voice. "You're engaged. I'm not the kind of person who does that. I barely know Brigette, but I'm not sure I can face her now."

"You were drunk and…" I decide it's better to leave out that she was depressed because she'll just deny it. "And I told you, I'm not going to tell her."

"Don't you see?" She ties the straw wrapper in a knot, pulling both ends to see if it breaks. She's been doing that since high school. It tears right in the middle of the knot, and she crumples it in her hand.

"Someone's thinking of you." I nod toward the now-balled white paper.

"I think I've just mastered how to pull the paper, so it breaks in the middle of the knot," she grumbles.

"No, it's because I'm always thinking of you."

She blows out a breath and sips her diet soda. "You can't say things like that."

"Why not? I'm your friend."

"My friend who's about to become someone's husband."

Usually I can figure out Juno, pull out a smile, but this marriage thing has erected a wall between us. Had I known I was going to lose my best friend… I shake my head. I need to remember that Juno refuses to ever cross that line.

"Can I ask you a question?" The good guy in me says not to ask. Don't be a dick right now. But the asshole part of me says it's time she realizes exactly what she did to us.

"What?"

The waitress slides our plates onto the table and Juno unwraps her silverware before crumbling her crackers into her soup.

"What did you think would happen when one of us got married? Or found someone serious?"

She drops her spoon into the soup.

"I mean, I tried to cross that line you put between us when we were thirteen many times. And I get it, Juno, you're scared. And I've allowed you to use that excuse because I don't know what it's like to lose my parents so young, but at some point, you have to live your life. You don't want to date me, but then no one else should have me?"

"I never said that. I'm happy for you. I am." Juno's jaw clenches. She swallows every time she lies.

"The way you've been acting the last six months since I got engaged says you're not."

She leans back and puts her hands in her lap. "I'm not used to sharing you. That's all."

"Exactly." I lean forward and my voice rises so loud that two employees at the counter glance over. "So I'll ask again, what did you think was going to happen when you were so hell-bent that we only ever remain friends?"

She balls up the napkin and throws it on the table. "I wasn't expecting to feel so left behind, okay? I didn't think. Is that what you want to hear?"

Now the employees are blatantly staring, as are most of the people in the diner.

She slides out of the booth. "I didn't think I'd lose you, and I was stupid for thinking that. You have another woman in your life now. I'm second, so if you could please give me a little time to get used to that thought rather than throwing accusations at me, I'd appreciate it. It's not like you've been entirely gracious when I've dated in the past either."

Then she's out. I have no energy to chase her, so I let her go, but my mind can't help drifting back to the last time she said she felt left behind.

SEVEN

Colton

Thirteen years old

My mom's sniffling echoes in my ear as her hand tightly grips mine. Everyone in Lake Starlight is holding their loved ones closer these days after the deaths of Tim and Beth Bailey. Typical small-town mentality says that something like this doesn't happen here, but it did.

My family, along with a lot of Lake Starlight, sits across from the Bailey kids and their grandma at the burial plot. Some people chose only to attend the church service.

The woman behind me whispers to her husband that Denver's missing. I noticed that too, but more because they left the chair between Juno and Rome empty. Whether it was planned or not, I don't know, but they sat in birth order.

The dark sky over the cemetery feels like a sign that we're all mourning the deaths of Tim and Beth Bailey.

Their snowmobile crashed into a tree, and neither of them survived their injuries after being rushed to the hospital.

My mom hasn't stopped crying since we got the news. Still, she and Mrs. Kelly set up a dinner delivery service to the Bailey house to make sure the kids don't starve. Although their grandma isn't old, she's not young enough to care for the seven of nine children who still live at home. Which is what has everyone asking... who will raise the Bailey kids and run Bailey Timber?

Sedona scurries out of her chair and climbs into Savannah's lap. Austin and Rome look as if they're seconds from crying based on their trembling chins. Kingston is openly sobbing with his arm slung over Phoenix at the end of the line. I'm focused on Juno, who sits in her chair with her legs crossed and not one tear falling down her cheeks.

The double black caskets are covered in an array of pastel-colored roses with Mr. and Mrs. Bailey's wedding picture on an easel between them. The preacher continues his speech about grief and how we can honor them through our memories. Austin leans forward, resting his forearms on his thighs, and I watch intently to see if he's finally going to break.

My mom squeezes my hand tighter and a howling sound escapes her as the preacher finally finishes his speech about how the Baileys will be watching us like angels and that they couldn't live on this Earth without each other, so God took them together. Then he excuses us and says the family would like some private time.

A lady from the church hands each kid two roses of a different color.

All the guests walk down the steep hill, but I keep looking over my shoulder to check on Juno.

My mom stops to talk to Mrs. Johnson, carrying on

about how sad it is and asking if anyone has heard whether their grandma will raise them. Austin's due to graduate from college in May and there're rumors about him being drafted to play in the pros. Savannah's only nineteen, but maybe she'll return from college as well. They talk about Bailey Timber and who will run the family business. They make it all sound so hopeless, that the Bailey kids have nothing now.

I stray away from my parents, walking up the hill enough to get a better view of the Baileys. Liam Kelly's leaning under a tree and I pause a few feet from him. He quickly swipes at his face when he notices me. How can a guy that big, the guy who gets into fights, cry?

We watch each kid put a rose on each casket. Savannah gently lays hers down while Rome tosses his in. Then they join hands and circle the caskets with their grandma and the preacher. We can't hear what is said, but all their heads bow, and when they rise, all of them are crying. Well, all of them except Juno. Austin swipes his tears with his palm, looking around at his siblings as though he needs to remain tough being the oldest.

"They'll need us, you know?" Liam says. "We have to be the best damn friends they could ever have."

I nod. "I know."

The Bailey kids break apart, and Savannah walks down the hill first, Sedona and Phoenix on either side of her and holding her hands. Brooklyn follows, patting her face with a Kleenex while Austin and Rome are behind her. Then Juno and Kingston bring up the rear. Her arm is around her younger brother, who looks as if he's barely hanging on as he glances back over his shoulder at the caskets. As they get halfway down the hill, Kingston runs back up and lays himself over his mother's casket.

It feels as though it all happens in slow motion. Juno calling out to Austin. Austin stopping and looking back. His quick jog back up the hill. As soon as he picks up Kingston and holds him, the moms still lingering around whimper. Kingston hits Austin with his fists to try to get down. I look around and see everyone watching the scene unfold. It's heartbreaking that the Bailey kids have to live through this with a spotlight on them.

"Well, shit," Liam says, his chin falling to his chest.

Austin holds Kingston and sets him on a bench that faces the caskets as Savannah organizes the rest of the kids into the awaiting cars.

As if that's the cue for all the gawking bystanders, Liam and I get called over by our parents. On my way to my parents' car, I watch Juno stare one more time at her brothers on the top of the hill before she slides into the back seat of the car. Still not one tear.

Although there aren't a lot of words shared between Liam and I, we share the same goal—be there for the Bailey kids from this day forward.

AN HOUR LATER, we're at the Bailey house. My mom is in the kitchen, distracting herself by refilling serving platters and cleaning. Mrs. Kelly is there too, but every time I go in the kitchen, she's staring out the window, washing a dish.

I've looked everywhere for Juno since I got here and nothing.

Denver finally showed up, and he's playing basketball in the driveway with Rome and Liam. Kingston is pretty much following Austin around, and Phoenix and Sedona are playing games in the basement with the other kids.

Brooklyn is with her group of friends on the back porch while Savannah makes the rounds and talks to each of the guests, reassuring everyone that they are fine, and it will all work out.

When I walk around their house and spot the treehouse, I could hit myself in the forehead. The treehouse is where Juno hides when she wants to be alone. That summer when the family joke was that Juno wasn't a real Bailey because of her red hair, she ran off in the middle of a barbeque and hid up there. Mrs. Bailey followed and got her to come back down an hour later.

"Juno," I say, calling up. The ladder has been taken up, which is a dead giveaway that she's up there.

Nothing but silence.

"I know you're up there. Come on."

Still nothing, so I look at my khaki pants and button-down shirt. My mom will be pissed if I ruin them, but what choice do I have? I scale the tree and climb in through a window.

"Colton." She sounds upset, but she doesn't tell me to leave. Her black shoes lay haphazardly in the corner as though she flung them off the minute she got up here.

"Have you eaten?" I should've brought her food.

"Not hungry." She stares at the picture of her Aunt Etta while she bounces a ball across the small space. Ever since the talk with her mom, that picture has hung in the treehouse. Along with astrology books and books on reading palms and other crap that doesn't interest me.

"Do you need anything?" I ask.

She looks up from bouncing her small ball. "What did you think about our kiss?"

That's not the question I thought would come out of her mouth. I've guiltily thought about the kiss the past few days. Hell, I've even envisioned more happened between us.

"It was nice," I say.

"Nice?" She obviously doesn't like me using that word. "You don't say nice to describe a kiss, Colton."

I shrug. "I liked it."

"Me too." She goes back to bouncing her ball. "But it can never happen again."

I'm nodding until I register her words, then I stop. "What? Why?"

She tosses me the ball and I catch it before throwing it back to her. "Do you remember how close Savannah was to Jeremy Crandle? They were inseparable. I overheard her talking to her friends on the phone last year and she told them that she finally kissed him. That was it—Jeremy Crandle was never seen again."

"Doesn't he live in New York or something?" There were a lot of rumors about Jeremy Crandle. Maybe Savannah wasn't his type only because she was a girl.

"Exactly. So me and you? Friends forever and never more. Okay?" She grabs the ball and tucks it into the skirt of her dress.

"Did you not like the kiss?" I ask. She can tell me. I might ask her to be my practice buddy, but I want her to tell me before I play another game of Spin the Bottle.

Her cheeks flush like they did that night in her basement. "I did, but I can't bear to lose someone else." A tear slips from one eye then another.

"But I…" Another tear falls and I stop talking.

The moment I've been waiting for is happening and I'm alone with no one else to comfort her. I look through the window and no one is in the backyard. I slide closer to her and put my arm around her shoulders.

She buries her head into my neck, her fingernails clawing at my shirt as if a black bear is ready to attack us. "They left me. How could they leave me?"

I hold her while her tears soak my shirt.

As the sun sets and the air gets cooler, Grandma Dori yells from the bottom of the tree. "*Juno!*"

Juno straightens her back, swipes her tears away, and puts on an act. "Yes, Grandma?"

"Come eat now, you've been up there long enough."

"Coming." She hurriedly puts her shoes back on, struggling with the small buckle until I finally take over and do it for her. "Friends forever, right?"

I nod and she smiles, tossing the ladder through the opening and climbing down from the treehouse.

Once she's gone, I whisper, "But what if I like you more than a friend?"

EIGHT

Juno

On Saturday evening, I walk out of my room and find Kingston sitting on the couch, gaming. Since it's spring and he works as a smoke jumper, in a few weeks, he'll probably be gone more than he's home.

He looks me up and down with raised eyebrows. "Where are you going?"

"I have a date." I walk over to my purse and shove my lipstick into the clutch.

Brooklyn has the perfect crossbody purse to go with my outfit, but I didn't call her to borrow it because I haven't told anyone I'm going on a date. Mostly because they'll look at me like Kingston is right now. That look that says, "What the hell are you doing, Juno?"

"Not with Colton?" He's turned back to his game now, his thumbs pressing buttons a million times in a row. Obviously, from the shorts and shirt he's wearing, he's not planning on going out tonight.

"I assume Colton is going out with his soon-to-be wife." I slide into the kitchen, needing to get rid of the nerves that won't stop making me feel as though my salad from lunch wants to come back up. I haven't been on an actual date in a long time. Trey wasn't a date; he was a hook-up. A mistake, really, because I didn't think I'd have to see him in Lake Starlight as much as I do.

I crack open a beer and come back into the room.

"You haven't shut that down yet? I thought maybe you guys figured your shit out the night of the baby shower." His eyes stay fixed on whatever war game he's playing.

"I wouldn't sleep with someone who's getting married." I act offended, but the truth is I would have, and I can't get over what a horrible person I am for that.

He tosses the controller next to him on the couch. "Fuck. I'm dead."

Standing, he disappears into the kitchen and, from the sound of it, gets himself a beer.

He sits back down and stares at me. "So who's the new guy?"

That's the Kingston we all know and love. He never digs too deep into any of our business. Just prods our shells gently in case we feel like opening up and talking. Sometimes I think he doesn't push because he doesn't want the questions poised back at him.

"A guy who came in to be matched," I say.

"I thought rule number one was not to date the clients?" He tips back his beer, then grins.

"Well, I'm amending that rule for when you feel sorry for yourself and a guy seems pretty smitten with you. I need to move on with my life. I mean..." Sometimes

Kingston is so easygoing, he makes it too comfortable to unload on him.

"I'm not quite sure you understand that you're not hiding your feelings for Colton from anyone. Maybe they're new to you, but all of us have always known."

I throw the beer cap at him and he catches it flawlessly. Too bad he couldn't have continued with baseball and gone pro like Austin wanted him to do instead of endangering his life every smoke jumping season as though he doesn't care whether he lives or dies.

"What happened to my brother who doesn't want to talk about shit? You just threw two axes my way. You trying to open me up?"

He chuckles and sets his beer on the table, lifting his phone from the table. "I like Colton and I think you're making a huge mistake by letting him marry that French chick."

"Her name is Brigette."

"Her name should be stuck in the middle. She probably has no idea what she's in the middle of between you two. It's always been you and Colton. Hell, he taught me how to shave. Remember that?"

I laugh because I remember when Colton offered without me even asking. Austin was so busy raising all of us and the twins were causing trouble somewhere and Kingston was being made fun of about his barely-there mustache. "I do."

"I still managed to cut myself five times."

"Maybe he wasn't that good of a teacher."

"I think if you really dig deep, you're going to figure out the date you should be on tonight is with Colton."

"Are you attending psychology classes in your free time?"

He shakes his head and picks up his phone. "Nah, but I have a lot of time for self-examination in my job. I think I'm growing up even though you guys still think of me as some ten-year-old."

I finish my beer as the buzzer of our door rings.

Kingston stands. "I got this."

"You're going to act like the overprotective brother?" I follow him to the door.

"For Colton's sake. Yes." He presses the buzzer with a, "*What?*"

I roll my eyes.

Kingston presses the button to let in my date. I forgot I had wanted to ask Kingston something else. I thought of a way to salvage my business since I'm now going on a date with my only potential client.

"Hey, I was thinking that to drum up some business, maybe I'd host a speed dating night up in Anchorage. Try to get some more business there."

"Lame," Kingston says.

"Lame? What's lame about that?"

"Because we're not in the eighties anymore. No one wants to go to a bar and be forced to talk to someone they don't like for five minutes."

The knock on the door makes the nerves in my stomach rumble.

"I'll think of something though," Kingston says, straightening his back and puffing out his chest.

He opens the door. Jason stands there looking a lot like he did the day he came into my office, except his jeans aren't as worn, and instead of a T-shirt, he's wearing a button-down with the arms rolled up to his elbows.

"You want to date my sister?" Kington asks.

I mouth "sorry" behind his back.

"I'm Jason." He puts out his hand.

Kingston shakes it. I should tell my brother he's not very intimidating without his smoke jumper outfit.

"Kingston. Juno's brother." He steps aside and Jason walks in.

Our apartment is small. Two bedrooms, a living room, dining area, and galley kitchen. We share a bathroom, but Kingston's not here for weeks at a time, so that makes it easier. I feel a little self-conscious though. I'm sure Jason has some great place since he's an eye doctor.

"Nice to meet you," Jason says before his gaze lands on me. "Hey, Juno. You look great."

I opted for a spring dress and a jean jacket. It's nice outside, but the nights still get pretty cold. "Thank you. You too."

I look at Kingston when he fails to leave us alone. He's not exactly the intimidating presence he thought he could be. Then again, he's never been the overprotective brother to me. I never gave him much reason to be one either.

"We should go," I say, eyeing Kingston.

"Nice to meet you," Jason says to him once we're on the other side of the door.

"Can't say the same." Kingston taps the edge of the door and it shuts in our faces.

He didn't just do that. My brother was brought up with manners.

"I'm sorry." I give Jason an embarrassed smile.

Jason returns my smile and opens the door to go down the stairs to the outside. "It's okay. I have a little sister too."

"I'm the older sister."

"Well, I guess a sister is a sister and you have to protect them."

I walk down the stairs, careful not to slip in my boots. "Where did you want to go?"

"I made reservations at a restaurant called Terra and Mare. It's in the downtown area, so we don't have to drive, and they opened up a garden dining area outside."

I inhale a breath. I should've put some stipulations on this date. "Um..."

He stops us before we cross the street. "Is that a problem? Do you not like the food there? I'm sure I can cancel, although they said if I—"

"Cancel within two hours of your reservation, you're charged fifty dollars," I say.

He nods. "Yeah, but if you don't like the place, I'll eat the money."

I don't want to be a problem, so I tug on his sleeve. "No, but lucky you, you get to meet two of my brothers in the same night."

He chuckles, but it has an *oh shit* edge to it, as though he'll gladly eat the fifty dollars knowing that. "Oh?"

"My other brother owns Terra and Mare. If we're lucky, he won't be there." But it's Saturday night—I know he will.

Jason falls in line and doesn't argue.

Walking into Terra and Mare, I spot Harley at the hostess station. This is going to suck.

"Juno?" she asks, looking quickly at my date.

"Hey, Harley, this is Jason."

Harley smiles and they exchange pleasantries. Her stomach isn't showing yet and I'm really hoping since she's here, Rome's not.

"Rome taking care of the kids?" I ask, showing Jason my fingers crossed behind the hostess stand.

"No. Phoenix and Griffin have them at their house. They're doing some outside movie thing and we weren't going to turn down free babysitting. But then our hostess called in and the chef in training isn't doing things the way Rome wants, so this is our night."

"Okay, can you sneak us out onto the patio? Jason has a reservation." I rise up on the balls of my feet and point at his name on her electronic screen.

"You don't want to be on the patio tonight. It's so cloudy," she says quickly.

"It's beautiful, and I'd much rather be out there than in here." So close to Rome.

"Nah. I have a perfect table right by the window." She points to said table for two.

"I think I picked the patio when I reserved online," Jason says.

Harley smiles at him and glances over her shoulder. "You know we have this special dessert, but it involves fire and it's so windy outside that those customers aren't being offered it. Juno loves her sweets."

"Thanks for that, Harley, but I think we'll go ahead and eat outside." She stares at me long and hard, and I try to decipher what she's trying to tell me. "Oh, is Grandma Dori here?" I whisper.

Harley shakes her head as if we're playing a game of charades.

Jason's hand lands on the small of my back because he's ready for Harley to escort us outside, but she's yet to grab the menus. "Can we be seated now?"

Harley blows out a breath, and I hope this is just some sort of pregnancy brain thing going on with her. She picks up two menus. "Of course. I'll have Rome come over and visit."

"Oh no, that's okay. He already met Kingston," I say.

"Kingston doesn't scare anyone," she says.

"He can be rude though."

Harley glances back at me as though she doesn't understand. She opens up the door to the patio, allowing us to go first.

"Thanks," I say.

"I tried to tell you," she whispers.

My gaze shifts from her to the small patio with eight tables—where Colton and Brigette are drinking wine at a table for two.

My feet stop and Jason bumps into my back. I scramble to turn around, my hands landing on Jason's chest, which is completely inappropriate for a date that only started minutes ago. "I changed my mind. It's way too cold outside."

"It's beautiful," Jason says.

"I tried to warn you. Now you can have that dessert. Rome made it for me last night. You're going to love it." Harley wedges herself between the inside and the patio, holding the door open for us to move back inside, but Jason isn't budging.

"Yes, and Harley's right. I love sweets. So much you'd think I'd be a diabetic. But I'm not. Not that all diabetics love sweets. Bad example. But sugar is my kryptonite." I push Jason, who doesn't give an inch.

"Juno?"

My forehead falls to Jason's chest and my hands fist his shirt. It's over.

I look up and Jason is staring at my hands. I release the fabric of his shirt and smooth it to get the wrinkles out. "I'm so sorry."

After a second or more, Harley says, "Juno."

I remove my hands off his chest, turn around, and smile. "Brigette."

Colton stares behind me, his jaw tense.

"Come and join us. Harley, can we have a table for four?" Brigette doesn't need Harley though because she's already taking the table next to hers and sliding it across the concrete, interrupting everyone's meal with the screechy sound.

I sit down next to Brigette because she's patting the chair nonstop and I look at Colton. It's bad enough that we got into a fight earlier this week and haven't talked. Now I have to share my dinner date with him.

Harley shoots me an expression wishing me luck when she hands us the menus. Boy, do I need it.

NINE

Colton

Juno smiles at Brigette and Brigette smiles back as though this is the best thing ever. She was mentioning to me how we should double date at some point with another couple. I said sure—but the last person I want to do that with is Juno.

"I'm Colton." I put out my hand in front of the guy next to me.

"Oh sorry." Juno shakes her head. "Jason, this is Colton and Brigette. This is Jason. He's from Greywall."

"Nice to meet you," Brigette says.

He shakes my hand and makes eye contact, but his grip could be firmer if you ask me.

"Are you French?" Jason asks Brigette hearing her accent.

Here we go. Another conversation about the Eiffel Tower and the Louvre.

"I am."

"What area are you from?" Jason asks.

"Marseille," Brigette says.

His face lights up. "Really? I backpacked through Europe with some buddies after high school. We went all through the Calanques National Park."

Now it's Brigette's eyes lighting up. She leans forward, her hand touching him because she talks with her hands nonstop. The two of them talk about Brigette's town in the south of France while Juno buries her head in the menu as if she hasn't eaten everything on there ten times over.

"Do you want me to trade spots?" I ask Jason. More so I have a reason to be across from Juno because then we can at least maybe have a civil conversation.

"Nah." He looks at Juno. "Sorry, it's just I've always said I'd go back there but never made it."

"I'm hoping to drag this one over there this Christmas." Brigette touches my arm. "So he can meet my family."

Juno peeks up, catches my eyes, then looks at the menu again. "They're not coming to the wedding?" She glances at Brigette only.

"No. Too hard to get away and it's such a long trip. We figure we'll marry here and then do another ceremony in front of my parents in France."

"That's a shame," Juno says.

"You two are getting married?" Jason asks.

Brigette holds up her left hand where a conservative white gold band with an average-sized diamond rests.

"Congratulations," he says. "When's the big day?"

"In three weeks," Juno answers.

Brigette glances from her to me with a questioning look as if she's missed something. I shrug.

"Let's order," I say, raising my hand for the waitress.

"Oh, I haven't even looked yet." Jason picks up his menu. "What do you suggest, Juno?"

She shrugs. "I'm sure you'll love anything. My brother's an excellent chef."

As though he heard his name, Rome walks out onto the patio. He stops at a few tables on the way to us, asking if they're enjoying their meals. He laughs with a few customers and thanks everyone wishing him congratulations on the new baby because that hit Buzz Wheel the minute Harley bought a test at Don't Be A Pill Pharmacy. Good thing that was the same day the news came out at the triple baby shower. They'll be up to four kids and it still feels like Harley just popped into town sometimes.

"Juno." Rome nods to his sister and eyes Jason.

I guess I should feel fortunate, since I've been a pseudo-Bailey my entire life, her brothers never gave me the third degree about anything.

"And you are?" Rome asks Jason.

"Give it a rest," Juno mumbles.

"Hi." Jason slides out his chair and slides his hand into Rome's. "I'm Jason."

Rome shakes his hand. "Hey, Colton, Brigette."

Juno sighs.

Then she looks up to see if anyone heard her, but Rome quickly intercedes. He's either covering for his sister or didn't hear it. "How about the special tonight?"

Juno shuts her menu. "Done."

"What's the special?" Jason asks.

Rome stares at him so long and hard that I actually squirm in my chair. "A shrimp pasta with pesto."

Jason looks concerned. "I've never had pesto."

"Oh, it's really good. Rome is the only one who makes it just like it is in Italy. Must be the name." Brigette winks.

"Well, there's a reason for that." When she looks at him blankly, Rome continues, "It's where I was conceived."

"Really?" Brigette says.

Juno groans.

"You don't know?" Rome asks. "I guess you're not from Lake Starlight."

"What? What?" Brigette bounces in her chair like a kid asking her parents what the big surprise is.

"We're all named after the places where we were conceived," Juno says in a monotone voice.

"They spelled your name wrong," Jason says to Juno.

She shoots him the death glare that's been aimed in my direction for most of the night.

"Unless there's another Juno I don't know about?" Jason looks at us as though he's expecting one of us to save him.

"Austin, Texas. Savannah, Georgia. Brooklyn, New York. Denver, Colorado. Rome, Italy. Juno—Wait? You're twins, right?" Brigette asks Rome.

Rome sets his hand on the back of Juno's chair. "To answer the first question, they did spell Juno differently because she's always been the unique one in our family. The only one with red hair." He nods down to her, and I watch her swallow down the lump in her throat. "And it was a layover in Denver on their way to Rome. It could be that I should be Denver and he should be Rome but..."

Brigette laughs and nods. "What about Kingston?" She looks at me. "Where's that from?"

"Jamaica," I say.

Brigette elbows Juno. "Your parents really got it on, huh?"

Juno smiles, but it slips right off her face when she turns away from Brigette. "Yeah, they did."

"Rome's following in their footsteps. Harley is pregnant with number four already," Brigette says.

Speak of the devil, Harley comes outside, and Rome slides his arm around her waist, kissing her temple. "If we're lucky."

"Lucky for what?" she asks.

"To have nine kids like my parents."

Harley smacks his stomach and shakes her head.

"Nine?" Jason coughs out his water. "You come from a family of nine? I didn't realize there were nine of you."

Rome's eyes scrunch. "Where are you from?"

"Greywall," Jason answers, pride in his tone. He obviously didn't grow up in Greywall because the Bailey name is well-known.

"You should move to Lake Starlight," Rome says. "Greywall sucks."

"How long does the pesto meal take?" Juno asks, and Rome's gaze falls to hers.

"I'm sure Rome can put a rush on it," Harley says. "Actually, I think Len was struggling a little bit in the kitchen."

"Okay." Rome knocks his knuckles on the table. "Nice meeting you, Jason. I should give you hell because Juno's my sister, but I think the guy to your right will take care of that for all us Bailey men. Right, Colton?"

Jason's and Brigette's heads turn toward me. Juno rolls her eyes. If I had my way, he wouldn't even be here. I'd have some magic powers to make him disappear.

"Why did he say that?" Jason asks Juno.

She sits up straighter in her chair and her gaze darts from me to Jason. "We're childhood friends."

"Childhood?" Brigette asks.

So I haven't been completely honest with her about

Juno. She knows we're good friends, but maybe not how long we've been friends.

"Yeah. She's my best friend," I say in the hopes that Juno will remember why we're friends. Forget the fight at the diner and move on.

"Best?" Brigette asks, her gaze volleying between Juno and me.

"Yeah, I've seen him at his worst. To me, he's just a kid with chicken legs and Oreos stuck in his braces." Juno laughs.

"And I knew her when she was still stuffing her bra," I say, hammering back an equal insult.

"Oh, so you're really close." I hear in Brigette's tone that she's silently asking if this is something she should worry about.

Juno puts her hand on Brigette's shoulder. "He's just like another one of my brothers."

Brigette's vision shifts to me and I force a smile although it feels as if someone shot me in the heart with a dagger.

Our salads arrive and Rome sends over a complimentary bottle of wine. While Jason concentrates all his attention on Brigette, going back to their conversation about Marseilles, I pull my phone out of my pocket.

Me: *I'm sorry. Forgive me?*

Brigette glances at me and I mouth "work" to her. Lying doesn't feel good, but the way Brigette asked about Juno and me being close friends says I made the right choice when I originally described our friendship to her.

"Oh, hold on one sec," Juno says, pulling out her phone when it dings.

Neither Jason or Brigette give her a second glance,

talking about boat rides or castles or something. I watch Juno as I fork my salad, her two thumbs poised over the phone. My phone vibrates in my pocket.

Juno: *I'm sorry too. I'll try harder.*

Me: *I know this is different.*

Juno: *She's nice. I'm glad you found someone so nice.*

Although that empty pit that's resided in my stomach all week disappears with her forgiveness, things are still awkward. But I guess I have to assume that's the way it will be now.

Me: *Jason's nice.*

I really need to stop lying so much.

Juno: *He is, and he seems very into your fiancée.*

I look up from my phone and see that neither of them have touched their salads. You'd think the two of them were on a date.

Me: *Maybe we should leave and see if they even notice?*

Juno: *:P We should probably try to join the conversation.*

Before I can respond, Juno puts her phone back inside her purse. I guess that's the end of that.

"Who was that?" Brigette asks the minute I put my

phone away. I knew she saw the exchange. She's got the vision of a sharpshooter.

"It was Mrs. Lopez about her cat," I say.

She nods because Mrs. Lopez calls every other day about some new ailment she thinks her cat has.

The waitress arrives with our main dishes and it's only then Jason realizes he never ate his salad, so we all shift around the plates so that he and Brigette can eat their salads with their pasta.

"This is so yummy. It must have been wonderful growing up with Rome cooking for you," Brigette says to Juno.

"He's only a year older than me, so we were grown before he could really cook me a meal that wasn't mac and cheese."

"Oh yeah," Brigette says. "I guess I didn't realize you were so close in age. Maybe because he's married with kids, he seems older."

I inwardly cringe as I twirl my fork around the pasta.

"Yeah, I'm just the loser sister," Juno says.

Jason says nothing, finally eating his salad.

"Oh, I didn't mean it—"

"I know. It's fine. Sorry. I'm not being very good company tonight." Juno twirls her own fork.

I'm hoping Rome's pesto will help boost Juno's mood. I've witnessed her mood change with a slice of pizza or a handful of fries.

Brigette shoots me an apologetic look and I shake my head.

"You guys were right. This is so good." Jason's fork is full of noodles as he's still chewing. "How have I never had this before?"

"Don't think you can get it just anywhere either,"

Brigette says. "We tried that place in Anchorage, remember, Colton?" Her nose crinkles and she shakes her head.

I catch Juno rolling her eyes. Rome's pasta isn't doing the trick.

"Um." Jason clears his throat. "Is this..." He clears his throat again. "There aren't nuts in this dish, right?" He points at the dish before grabbing his throat.

"Pine nuts," Brigette says, apparently more familiar with what goes into the dish than I am.

Juno's eyes widen. "You're allergic?" Her chair scrapes along the concrete.

All the tables around us turn their attention to ours.

"We need a doctor," Brigette says.

"Do you have an EpiPen on you?" Juno asks Jason, whose face is growing red and swollen and is fumbling with his hand in his pocket.

Jason nods his head. Juno's eyes widen, silently asking me what to do.

"Grab it and stab him in the leg with it then let's get to the hospital," I say, pulling my keys out of my pocket. What kind of idiot doesn't tell the restaurant they have an allergy?

Jason pulls his EpiPen from his pocket and manages to stab himself in the thigh with it. We all run, Juno screaming to Harley about the bill. Jason slides into the back seat of the truck and Juno sits in the passenger seat, leaving Brigette standing by the door.

"Right. Sorry." Juno climbs down and into the back seat with Jason.

Our eyes lock through the rearview mirror briefly. I guess I never did realize how different things would be.

TEN

Juno

"Y ou guys should go," I say to Brigette as we wait for Colton, who went down to the vending area to grab drinks and snacks. We've been here for hours already.

Since I'm not immediate family, I have no idea how Jason's doing.

Talk about an epic fail of a date. First, I'm fairly sure he wished he was on a date with Brigette, then he has an allergic reaction and ends up looking like Will Smith in that movie *Hitch*.

"No." Brigette crosses her legs. She smiles at me from her magazine. "We're all in this together."

I sit in a chair, pick up a magazine, then realize it's *Sports Illustrated*, so I toss it back onto the table. The only other person in the waiting room is an elderly man calmly reading a book in the corner. I don't recognize him. I wonder if he's from Lake Starlight?

"Can I ask you a question?" Brigette shuts her magazine.

"Sure."

"Is that why you've been cold to me? Because you don't think I'm good enough for Colton?"

Oh shit, I cannot have this conversation right now. "No, I'm sorry. It's just been a lot with all my sisters having their babies."

"So you don't, like, have a thing for Colton? The two of you have never..."

Oh my God. We're going there? Right now? This day just keeps giving and giving.

"I've known Colton a long time and I can't lie and say things haven't happened between us before, but if we were meant to be together, we'd be together. You don't have anything to worry about."

A part of me wants to tell her the truth. That I convinced myself of the lie for so long that I didn't realize until she came along that I do want Colton. But I won't do that. I won't make trouble for Colton. I want him to be happy, and eventually, I'll accept that means that he's not with me.

"Okay. Well, if you're this close of friends, you should do something at the wedding."

"Um... no, that's okay."

She sits up straighter as if she's had an epiphany. "Yes. Could you read something? Colton wants it to be a super small ceremony and with my family not coming, we're not having anyone stand up for us, otherwise I'd just have you as a bridesmaid." I cough past the bile in my throat as she adds, "I already have almost everything arranged, but if you want to do a reading, let me know."

"That's okay. I'm not very comfortable talking in front of people."

She nods as if she really does understand. "Oh! We're taking dance lessons next week. Why don't you and Jason come? We can do a double date. I've been dying to meet some other couples."

I smile tentatively. "This was our first date and it ended with him in the emergency room. I'm pretty sure there won't be a second."

"Oh, I could tell he liked you." She smiles.

I think you're projecting, Brigette. "Yeah, I'm not sure."

"Come on. Colton keeps whining about going and maybe if you go, he'll be more into it."

"I doubt I'd make a difference." I pick up a magazine again and give it my full attention.

"Please," she says. "I really want to get to know you since you obviously mean a lot to Colton."

"We could just do lunch or something. Maybe just me and you?"

Bite your tongue, Juno. What the hell are you thinking? I'm thinking that the last thing I want to witness is her and Colton dancing. All I can envision is the movie *Dirty Dancing*. Which brings to the surface memories of how I made Colton practice that lift in the lake behind my house the entire summer when we were twelve.

"I'm not taking no for an answer. It will be fun. Give me your number," she says, phone poised in her hands.

Colton walks in with an armful of drinks and snacks. I widen my eyes at him, hoping he can distract his fiancée from wanting to become besties.

"What's going on?" He drops everything on the table.

"Brigette wants my number, and she'd like Jason and I

to go to your dance class next week," I say sweetly but hope that Colton catches on.

"We almost killed the guy. I doubt he'll want to go to a dance class with us."

Thank you, Colton.

She drops her phone, and the anxiety creeping up my spine dissipates.

"Well, we'll ask him." She leans forward, snagging my phone off the table. Brigette laughs and soon her phone dings. "Got your number now."

"Oh, you sneak you," I say, shooting a death glare at Colton. I'm putting a lock on my phone as soon as I leave here.

He raises his hands behind Brigette as though he has no control over her.

"Now we can plan that lunch and you can do the dance class with us."

I snag a bag of chips off the table. "Yay!"

I poorly feign excitement, but either Brigette doesn't care or she's oblivious. From what I've witnessed in the past, she's pretty smart, so I'm going with the former.

I'm just starting to nod off hours later when Jason walks into the waiting room. His shirt is untucked and wrinkled, and his hair is up in every direction.

Brigette stands before I get a chance. "Oh, Jason, how are you?"

Colton and I stand in unison and join them.

"Better now. Thanks." He runs his hand through his hair. "I guess I can't eat pesto."

Brigette laughs but stops when Jason doesn't.

"I'm really sorry," I say.

"It wasn't your fault. Mind if we head back to my car? I'm exhausted after all the medicine."

"Yeah, for sure. Do you want to leave your car at my place? I'm sure Colton could drive you back home," I say.

"To Greywall?" Colton says, and I smack his arm. "Sure. Yeah. No problem."

"That'd actually be great. I'm barely standing now. The stuff they give me makes me tired and jittery all at once. I'll grab an Uber in the morning for my car."

"Nonsense, we'll pick you up," Brigette cuts in.

Colton and I look at one another.

"I think we need a do-over," she says. "We can do breakfast."

"Um... I have a family dinner tomorrow." I raise my hand.

Brigette turns around. "I said breakfast."

Colton blows out a big breath. "Let's just get going. We can talk about it on the way."

Jason turns, and we file out of the waiting room as the older man winks at me. I stop momentarily, but he only smiles. I smile back and walk out of the room.

IT'S quiet and dark on the ride to Jason's. He's leaning his head against the window and Brigette's head is buried in her phone, the screen the only light in otherwise dark surroundings.

Colton's gaze keeps shifting from the road to the rearview mirror. He pulls to a stop at a light and the song "Like I Loved You" by Brett Young comes on the radio. My eyes lock with his in the mirror. The sadness I see in his cracks my heart open, but I'm not the one who's engaged to be married.

I tear my gaze away, and thankfully the green light

shines through the windshield. Colton presses on the gas, the GPS interrupting the song to give directions to Jason's house.

When Colton's truck rolls to a stop in front of a small two-story in downtown Greywall, I'm not surprised. He's so put-together, of course he's got a nice house with a perfectly manicured yard and white fence that's there more for aesthetics than anything. There's probably a golden retriever that was the star pupil in its obedience training class nestled in his designated dog bed inside too.

"Thanks a lot," Jason says, opening the door.

I slide out of the truck to help him up to his house. He opens the small gate, and we walk up the sidewalk to his front door.

"I'm sorry again," I say.

"It's okay, Juno. It wasn't your fault. I'm just exhausted. Can I call you tomorrow?"

"Are you sure you want to?" I wouldn't blame him if he didn't. One brother shut the door in his face, and another almost killed him.

"Yeah." He glances at the truck. "I'll call you tomorrow and we'll figure out a date."

I nod and rise up on the balls of my feet to hug him— which should make me feel better because this has been the worst date I've ever been on and nothing horrible even happened to me. He hugs me back then puts the key into the lock.

I fall back down to my heels, quickly turning to the sidewalk. "Have a great night."

"You too."

I walk toward Colton's truck, silently lecturing myself to get my shit together. Colton is getting married whether I like it or not. I shouldn't let a good guy like Jason slip through my fingers. I need to stop wallowing. My business is in the red and I need it back in the black. So what if Kingston thinks speed dating is eighties? It'll get me business.

Without warning, my legs get taken out from under me and I fly up in the air before landing on Jason's lawn.

"*Juno!*" Colton jumps out of the truck.

"Rufus!" Jason shouts, but it's too late—I'm being licked by a hundred-pound dog on top of me. "I'm sorry," he says.

"You should get him trained." Colton grabs the dog's collar and pulls him off me so I can stand.

Jason's takes the dog from Colton. "He is trained. He must like you." Jason smiles at me.

I roll onto my knees and pet Rufus, who keeps trying to climb me like a fire hydrant. I guess I had it wrong—Rufus wasn't the star pupil of his class.

"I'll give you a number for a better dog trainer." The angry edge to Colton's voice is unnecessary. I'm fine.

Brigette rolls down the window. "Everything okay?"

I stand and brush off my butt. "We're good. Let's go. See you another time, Rufus." I pet his head before walking to the sidewalk.

Colton puts his arm around me to help me as if I have injuries from the fall. I don't say anything until my eyes land on Brigette's. Her vision is focused solely on where Colton's hand is on my hip.

"I'm good, Colt, just knocked the wind out of me." I slide out from his hold and he opens up the truck door for me.

I climb in and he shuts the door, treating me as he always has, which I'm just now realizing is a lot like a girlfriend. We need to figure out this new normal between us.

Twenty minutes later, after a ride in a deadly silent

truck, I'm dropped off at my house. I say goodbye, leaving them to do what people in love do. I guess I'll be digging into my bottom drawer again to please myself.

I open the apartment door and find Kingston still in his shorts and T-shirt, playing his damn video game. He takes a quick glance over at me.

"I thought for sure you wouldn't be home tonight..." His words trail off before he talks into the headset, flicking the buttons on the controller. "Damn it, Lou, cover me."

I go to the fridge and grab a beer and a slice of pizza that Kingston must have ordered tonight.

"Shit. I died. You're bad luck. Every time you walk into the room, I die." He tosses his headset and controller on the couch. "How much do you love me?"

I sit in the chair by the couch. "Enough that I won't tell anyone you willingly stayed home on a Saturday night by yourself."

"I have this friend at a bar in Anchorage. I called, and he said as long as it's during the week, you're golden. He's got a room in the back that can be sectioned off. And because you have an awesome brother, no charge. You can do your speed dating there, but I really think it should be blind speed dating."

My eyes widen. "Shut up, really?"

"How much do you love me now?" he asks with a grin.

"You're my favorite brother."

"Haven't I always been?"

I laugh. "Yeah. Of course." I hand him my beer since I haven't had any yet and go to get another one from the kitchen.

This is a lifesaver. For the first time in weeks, my body loses some of the tension it's been carrying around.

"Hey, King," I call.

"Yeah?"

"Thanks a lot."

He's silent for a moment. "That's what family is for."

I nod, my eyes watering. At least one thing tonight is heading in the right direction.

ELEVEN

Colton

When I arrive at the clinic on Monday, Brigette is sitting in the break room with her coffee, looking through her phone. She's been quiet this weekend, but I'm ignoring it rather than poking the bear.

"Good morning," I say.

"Good morning." She doesn't look up. "Dr. Murphy was looking for you earlier."

"Thanks." I change into my white coat and shut my locker. I'm about to leave the room, but I stop and put my hand on her shoulder. "You okay?"

She smiles at me and nods. "Yeah, why?"

"You've been quiet. Is it the wedding stress?"

She shakes her head. "No. You good?"

It's odd that she's asking me, but I smack on my smile. "Yeah."

We both nod as if we're the most agreeable people on

the planet and I head toward Dr. Murphy's office. His door is open, and Lori is sitting in the chair in front of him. She's leaning forward and whispering, a telltale sign that she's gossiping. Great.

"I took a screenshot," she says, giving her phone to Dr. Murphy.

He looks at it, shakes his head, and hands it back to her.

I knock on the open door and they both look at me. Lori's cherry-red cheeks say I'm the subject of said gossip. It wouldn't take Einstein to figure out that I must've been in Buzz Wheel last night.

That damn thing. I didn't check it on Saturday night nor last night, but I'm guessing from Dr. Murphy's concerned glare, I should have.

"Come in, Colton." Dr. Murphy waves me in.

He's only here three days a week now, and last year he discussed with me about investing in the business until I could buy him out completely. But I know a little birdie named Lori keeps whispering in his ear that I'm too young and the clients don't listen to me like they do him.

"Let me guess, I made Buzz Wheel?" I say just so Lori knows she doesn't need to go behind my back.

"You didn't see it?" She smiles sweetly at me. "That blog should be shut down. You can't even trust the information."

"Yet you take screenshots," I deadpan.

Her friendly demeanor fades. "I just think that Dick should know what's going on with his employees."

My gaze shoots to Dr. Murphy, and he pinches the bridge of his nose. "Lori, please give us a minute."

"Sure, I need to redo a file that got coffee spilled on it yesterday anyway." She stands and shoots me an accusatory glare.

I don't say so, but it was Brigette who spilled the coffee.

"I'm sure you wouldn't mind forwarding that Buzz Wheel to me?" I ask.

Her hand pauses on the door, but she doesn't turn around. "Of course, as soon as I get to my desk."

"Thanks."

She finally leaves and Dr. Murphy asks her to shut the door behind her, which means this is more serious than I thought.

"Colton, have a seat." He gestures, and I sit in the chair in front of his desk. I have an office, but mine doesn't have a window like his. I've mentally arranged my own furniture in this office many times. "I'm going to shoot straight, and I'd like you to be straight with me on a few things."

"Okay."

"I always thought of you as a Lake Starlight lifer. I started this practice five years after working in Anchorage for another veterinarian. You see the pictures on the wall. This place was small at first. One room, and now we have four rooms. It's not only Lake Starlight I see, but all the neighboring communities."

I lean back in the chair and rest my ankle on my knee. This is going to be a long conversation. I resist the urge to check my watch for fear of being rude. "Yes, you've done an amazing job."

"And when you came to me and asked to be an apprentice, I was thrilled. Mrs. Murphy and I not being blessed with our own kids, I knew one day I would have to make the tough decision about selling the practice. And I know we've talked about you buying a small stake, taking over day-to-day operations, and eventually buying out my share."

"Yes. I'm still very on board with that." I've never wavered.

"Things have changed though. You're getting married."

"To Brigette. I'm assuming she could stay on staff as well?" He's never had a problem with us before. Hell, the staff here had a cake to celebrate our engagement the day we announced it to them, so I'm not sure where he's coming from.

"Brigette is from France," he says as though I'm not aware.

"Yes, sir."

He opens his mouth as though to say something, then closes it before he says, "Are you sure she's not going to want to go back someday? What if she becomes homesick or wants a practice in a bigger city? You know being a veterinarian in a small town is very different than in a big city?"

"As far as I know, she wants to stay in Lake Starlight. She wants to make her life here."

He raises his eyebrows as though he's not so sure.

"Dr. Murphy, I assure you, if we go through with the plan of me taking over Four Paws, it's in good hands with me."

He straightens some papers on his desk. "That article Lori was just showing me says..."

"Says what? What could it possibly say?" My voice is louder than I'd like. Dr. Murphy doesn't respond when someone is argumentative, but this is pissing me off.

"It says what everyone in this town believes."

"Which is?" I clench my jaw.

He glances up from his papers. "That you're torn between two women. That Juno Bailey will always be your first love and Brigette is a replacement."

I shake my head.

"From my experience, with love triangles, sooner or later the one most affected flees just to get away from the situation. I'm not sure if Brigette reads that stupid gossip blog or not and I'd normally disregard it, but I've seen you with Juno. I've had a front row seat to your friendship all these years."

"Yeah, *friendship*," I say.

He raises his gray eyebrows once again. "From the picture on Buzz Wheel, I'd say you might need to reevaluate that again. Now." He holds up his hand. "I'm not saying that the deal is off the table. All I'm asking is that you think this through again. If you were marrying Juno, I'd have no concerns. Everyone knows she's not like her sisters Phoenix and Sedona. She's a lifer. But with Brigette, I'm not so sure she'll want to stick around. Especially if she has to put up with the constant rumors about your feelings for Juno."

"Dr.—"

"I don't want an answer right now. Discuss it with your fiancée. All I'm saying is I don't want to hand down the business to someone who will sell it off to someone else who will then sell to yet another person. I'd close it before I allowed it to be passed around."

I blink in surprise, never having heard him talk like that before. "I'm not sure how I'm supposed to prove this to you?" I crack my neck back and forth, my gaze straying to the window.

Harley's out there in the park with the kids and Rome's coming from Terra and Mare, walking over to join them. Phoebe runs to her dad, and he swings her around, her smile so wide I can see it from here. He wraps one arm around Harley, presses a kiss to her lips, then rubs her belly even though she's not showing yet. I'd be lying if I said my heart didn't pinch watching them.

"I'm a Lake Starlight lifer. I promise you," I say.

"Make sure Brigette is on the same page as you. And if you love her, I suggest closing that door to Juno, because speaking as a man who's been married for over fifty years, there can only be one number one woman in your life."

I nod. "So once I marry Brigette, we'll talk about me taking over Four Paws?"

"Yes, I'll have a conversation with her that should put me at ease if what you say is correct and she sees Lake Starlight as her new home. Then you and I will talk. After the wedding, of course. You have enough stress right now getting ready for the big day."

"Thanks, sir." I glance at my watch. "I've got to get to my first appointment of the day."

I'm at the door when he calls my name.

"Yes?" I turn and face him.

"Listen to your heart. That's the advice I was given a long time ago, and I promise you, your heart doesn't lie. It never leads you where you shouldn't go."

If he only knew that my heart has led me straight into heartache since I was thirteen.

"Thank you." I nod in appreciation and open the door just as Hillary is escorting my first client, Mrs. Lopez, and her cat, Alesander, to room two.

Knowing I have a few minutes, I pull out my phone to look at the text Lori sent me. Lake Starlight Buzz Wheel's glowing header hits me front and center.

Three to Tango?

RUMOR HAS it that Juno's date had an allergic reaction and somehow Colton Stone and his fiancée were the ones who drove them to the hospital. A source overheard Brigette asking Juno Bailey about her relationship with Colton. How close are they? Apparently, Juno claimed once again that they're just friends—not news to any of us. But the juiciest piece of information is that she said there have been times that the lines blurred between them. She assured the very jittery bride that if something were going to happen, it would have already, which apparently calmed Brigette down. We're also hearing that Juno will be attending dance lessons with the happy couple. Whose partner will she be?

This picture was taken when Juno's date finally emerged from the emergency room, recovered from his allergic reaction. As you can see, Juno and Colton are still side by side and it's Brigette's hand on Juno's date's arm. And where is Colton's arm? On the small of Juno's back. Tell me again that these two are just friends. I'm not buying it, and if I were Brigette, I'd get the hell out of Lake Starlight. Or maybe hit it with Juno's date, who she seems so fond of.

Colton Stone is due to wed in only three weeks... maybe we should open a pool to bet on whether it will actually happen.

I SCAN THE PHOTO. I can't deny that my hand is on Juno, but I've always been like that with her. Plus, I felt like after Brigette was so forceful about getting Juno's number and going to the dance studio, I wanted to convey to her that I was sorry. My guilt is always right under the surface since my engagement.

I pocket my phone as Brigette walks by me into exam

room three without saying a word. I guess I have my answer as to what was wrong with her this morning.

I HAVE no time to talk to Brigette all day until we're walking across the square to Tap Your Feet Dance Studio.

"Hey." I stop her before we cross the street. "I think we should talk."

"What about?"

"I'm pretty sure you saw Buzz Wheel."

Her smile drops. "I did, but it's fine. It's just gossip."

I want to talk this out, but she appears fine with ignoring the blinking neon elephant between us. "I still think we should talk."

She looks over my shoulder, her arm raised. "Later. They're here."

"Who?"

I turn and my eyes narrow. Juno and Jason are walking down the sidewalk toward us.

"I thought this was a no-go?" I ask through clenched teeth.

"I got a hold of both of them earlier. I thought you'd be happy that your best friend could make it today." A toddler could hear the sarcasm in Brigette's tone.

As Juno and Jason approach, the question begs to be answered. For whose benefit did she invite them: hers or mine?

TWELVE

Juno

Entering the dance studio above Sweet Suga Things, it's clear this was a bad idea. The only one comfortable one of us is Brigette, who is overly enthusiastic about the four of us double dating. I'm surprised Jason even agreed to go out with me again, but he's been nothing but courteous since he picked me up.

"Oh hi, Juno, how is everyone?" Mrs. Johnson asks when she spots me. "I saw Liam and Savannah the other day out on a walk. Liam said it was his first day back at work and he didn't want to leave them, so he convinced Savannah to bring the little one to visit." She chuckles.

"Yeah, I haven't had nearly the time I'd like to see the new babies." Which is true. Phoenix called me today, and I signed up for a shift on Thursday afternoon with Savannah. Phoenix said she might just knock Savannah out if she has to go over there again and be lectured on how to keep the changing area organized.

"They're only young once. Now, Mr. Johnson said you two were in and picked out Colton's suit already?" Yeah, Mrs. Johnson is Mr. Johnson's wife. She's only directing her attention to Colton and myself, which leaves Brigette and Jason to stand idly by like outsiders.

"I did," Colton says.

"And I heard Juno got a little gushy?" She touches my arm. "Now you see why we all cry when your brothers and sisters marry. When you've known someone and watched them grow, it's emotional."

I side-glance at Colton, who rocks back on his heels.

"I just made fun of his Oreo braces from when we were kids." I direct my response to Brigette, who gives me a small smile that barely lifts the corners of her lips. "Honestly, it wasn't like that, and my grandma—"

"Are you ready for us, Mrs. Johnson?" Brigette interrupts.

My shoulders fall. She's obviously upset, and I can't blame her. I saw the Buzz Wheel article Saturday night.

"Oh yes. You're a taskmaster, huh?" Mrs. Johnson pinches Brigette playfully, but Brigette stares at the spot on her arm. "That's a good quality, Colton."

Mrs. Johnson waves us into the studio that's lined with windows that face the square. The hardwood floors are shiny and polished, and there are benches along the interior wall—which look like a really good spot to lie down.

"You're all my early birds, so I'll put on some music and you can get those hips warmed up while we wait for the others."

"Great," I say without enthusiasm. If physical education

teachers could fail a student for their lack of rhythm, I would've failed square dancing.

She turns on Frank Sinatra's, "Fly Me to the Moon" and Jason holds out his arms to me.

"I should preface this by saying that I'm more of a side-step kind of dancer."

He laughs and wraps one arm around my waist while securing my hand in his. His form is rigid, so I try to do the same. "Just let me lead."

He steps forward—right on my toe because I guess I was supposed to step back.

"Sorry." I stare down at his feet.

"It's just a square," he says.

I follow him, feeling like a robot and stepping on his foot when we're supposed to go back. The last time I apologized so much was when I threw up in Liam's classic car my junior year, after I got wasted at a party.

"Now." He releases my waist, puts his finger under my chin, and brings up my face. "Your eyes stay on me. This is where the connection happens."

"Okay. Man, you're really good at this. Where did you learn?" Just as I think I can hold a conversation while dancing in a square, I mess up and my ankle twists.

"You okay?" he asks.

"Yeah. I'm fine." I stand up straighter to get back up on that horse, when really, I just want to leave. I'm not getting married. I don't have to dance at their wedding if I choose not to. Why did I agree to this? Oh yeah, because if Brigette is important to Colton, then she needs to be important to me, which means I need to do things like this to try to build a relationship with her.

"I'm a nerd and took ballroom dancing as a college cred-it," he confesses with a shy smile.

"Easy A?"

He chuckles. "Nope. The instructor made sure there wasn't anything easy about it. To pass the class, we had to partner up and do an actual dance contest."

"Whoa."

"Yeah, but she said I had hips for salsa. Whatever that means."

I glance down between us and see that as we step, his hips sway a little with each move. As if he's a chained up dog who wants to run free.

Meanwhile, Colton and Brigette dance next to us. Brigette seems to be doing okay while Colton silently counts with his mouth open.

"There you go," Brigette says. "You're kind of getting it, but more flair."

Colton tries, but he looks as if he's got ants in his pants. I laugh, causing him to look over at me and step on Brigette's toes.

"Damn it, can't you two be serious?" She unhooks herself from him and grabs her toe.

"Sorry," I say.

Two more couples come in. Mrs. Johnson says hello to them then comes over to us and puts her hands on my hips.

"More movement, Juno. Loosen up." Mrs. Johnson smacks my one hip as if it's fallen asleep. "There you go."

I feel no difference, but she leaves us alone, which I'm thankful for. Jason spins me, and I face Colton and Brigette.

"That was a nice move," I say to Jason, who smiles.

"Oh, I think we have a few dancers in the house," Mrs. Johnson calls. "I'm going to have you dance around with one another."

"I thought this was a party, let's dance!" Denver yells, entering the room with a red-faced Cleo.

I dislodge from Jason and cross my arms. *You've got to kidding me.*

"Who is that?" Jason asks.

"Um..."

"Denver Bailey, you do not enter a ballroom like that," Mrs. Johnson says.

"It's from *Footloose.*" He waits for her to show any recognition of the famous final line, but it never comes.

"I do not care. This is a ballroom." She takes his hand and leads him to the middle of the dance floor. "It is not to be knee in crotch and grinding."

Everyone laughs. I think she has her movies mixed up.

"All you had to do was ask, Mrs. Johnson." Denver brings her close and acts as if he's going to grind her.

She hits him but looks at Cleo, who's standing near the wall. "How are you ever going to marry this guy?"

"I guess I'm special because it takes a special girl to see his beauty." Cleo walks over and smacks him playfully, before taking the spot of Mrs. Johnson. Now Denver really does put his leg between her legs and grinds.

"Your cousin?" Jason asks.

I twist my lips into an apologetic expression. "Brother."

"Another one?"

"Yeah, but the last one you'd have to meet would be Austin and he's super chill."

"Just to be safe, let's dance on the other side of the room."

I laugh, thinking he's joking, but Jason really does spin me until we're in the opposite corner.

"Juno!" Denver yells, somehow dancing toward me.

"What on Earth are you two doing here?" I ask.

"Dance lessons for our wedding. Gotta start early. Plus,

we needed to get out of the house. Everyone's babies are ruining our social life." Cleo laughs.

"I'll put a baby in you," Denver says. "Let's ditch this class and go home and try until we're successful."

Cleo smacks him on the shoulder. "One hour. You promised."

Denver acts like a scorned puppy but his smirk is anything but.

"Let's switch partners. You have to be able to adapt when you dance. Allow the leader to lead you, then we'll start in on some steps." Mrs. Johnson comes around and pushes the couples apart.

I end up with Denver. Great. Colton is with Cleo, and Brigette and Jason are together. Immediately there's a visible difference in dancing capabilities between the couples. Jason and Brigette whizz around the dance floor as though they should be the instructors of the class, Brigette's skirt whooshing around her thin legs. I share a look with Colton. Yeah, we're the losers here.

"I didn't sign up to dance with my sister," Denver tells Mrs. Johnson, grabbing Cleo's hand and twirling her into his arms. "Sorry, sis."

That leaves me with Colton. We gravitate to the window, watching the other couples. The two other middle-aged couples seem comfortable swapping, which makes me wonder if they swap partners for more than just dancing.

"Oh no, you don't." Mrs. Johnson comes over and positions Colton and me into the classic dancing position. She puts his hand on my hip and locks our other hands together. "We're going to make you two dancers yet."

"It's just one dance. I can make it work," Colton argues, and she slaps his arm. "Firm. Strong." His eyes gravitate to Brigette and Jason, who are floating across the room.

"We're obviously the misfits of the group," I say.

"Not misfits. Just get out of that head of yours." Mrs. Johnson taps her finger to my temple. "Listen to the beat of the music. Let it be your guide. Get lost in your partner. It's not always about the perfect steps." She puts one hand on Colton's back and one on my mine, pushing us closer. "It's about enjoyment and passion. And whatever other emotions it pulls from you."

She leaves us to check on another couple. Colton steps much like Jason did but not nearly as smoothly. But I'm fine with that because I don't care as much if I step on Colton's toes.

"We've done this before," Colton softly says.

"What? Prom? We only danced to fast songs," I say.

I'm not sure he touched me that entire night. He went with Monica Lloyd and I went with Pete Segrum. It was the first school event we went to separately, but later that night, we met up. I'm not sure if that's what he's talking about or what.

"That night by the lake before I went to college," he says.

"That was a long time ago and we didn't have witnesses." I play off his comment as if that night is like any other one of our memories. Ones that don't pierce my heart because once again I'm losing him.

"Juno?" Colton has a specific tone he uses when he's obsessing over something. "We need to talk."

Our eyes lock. We can't cross that line now. We can't have the conversation I think he wants to have now.

I shake my head. "Later."

"I'll come by tomorrow at lunch," he says.

I nod although every cell in my body is screaming no, he's getting married.

"And switch!" Mrs. Johnson claps.

One of the middle-aged women slides between Colton and me while her partner puts his arms around me. But my eyes don't stray from Colton's and his don't leave mine.

All I can remember is that night before he left for Colorado State.

THIRTEEN

Juno

Seventeen years old

"Come on." I pull Colton down the pathway of our house toward the lake on our property.

"Why are we going to the lake? I thought we were going to watch *The Hangover?*"

I slide my arm through his and lean my head on his upper arm. He's grown so much through high school. The other day I noticed the way even his forearms are corded with muscles. He's going to forget me when he goes away to college.

"We will, but I want to give you a goodbye present."

"We wouldn't be saying goodbye if you would've come with me."

I look up at him and smile softly. Going to college together was the plan when we were young. But when my parents died, my plans changed. I can't leave Austin here alone to raise the twins.

We all get money for college or a business from my parents' inheritance, so I need to spend as little as possible so I have enough to start my matchmaking business. It just makes more sense for me to go to college here in Alaska.

"You'll be back. Lake Starlight is your home."

He nods. "Eventually, but if I don't end up going to vet school here, then we're talking eight years."

I shake my head. "Can we not talk about it right now?"

We arrive at the lake, the moonlight reflecting along the surface of the dark water. Small lanterns I put around a blanket at the edge of the water glow in the dark. My heart races as his footsteps fall to a stop and he looks at me.

"What's going on?"

I take his hand and lead him to the blanket. "I didn't want to just watch a movie in my basement where Kingston or the twins could come in and join us. I wanted to be alone with you."

A small smile tips his lips as though he's surprised that I would want that.

Just wait.

"I got all your Lake Starlight favorites. Strawberry pie from Lard Have Mercy, cookies from Sweet Suga Things, and Austin wants me to tell you it was him who went to Carol's Crabby Shack to pick up hushpuppies and crab legs."

I fall to my knees on the blanket, but Colton stays standing and takes in all the food and the lanterns.

"Juno." He shakes his head. "This is amazing." He drops to his knees and looks me in the eye. It spurs a rush of nerves. "Thank you."

"You're my best friend. Did you think I wouldn't do anything before you left?"

He shrugs. "I would've been happy to watch *The Hangover*. I just wanted my last night to be with you."

I push back thoughts of this being his last night in Lake Starlight. He's leaving me, but I want him to. Colorado State has always been his dream, and he deserves it and so much more.

"Let's eat before it gets too cold." I open up the takeout Austin picked up for me.

We eat in near silence except for the crickets making their music.

"Oh, I almost forgot." I abandon my food and walk over to the bench next to the lake.

My dad installed the bench for Grandma Dori because the lake is a place of reflection for my family. During family gatherings, she disappears here to think about my grandpa. I always wonder if I'll find the same kind of love that she shared with him.

I turn on the speaker so that music interrupts the crickets.

We eat our crab and talk about his new roommate, who he's talked to over the phone. He doesn't think he'll get along with him. I can tell how nervous Colton is to be away from home and not know anyone at his new school. We promise to write letters, emails, and text all the time. And we count how many days he'll be gone before he returns for the short Thanksgiving break.

After we're both full from our dinners, "Need You Now" by Lady Antebellum comes on the radio and Colton stands, holding his hand out for me.

"Dance with me," he says.

"I can't dance." I shake my head, cleaning up our containers.

"As a gift to me?"

"Hey, I got you that nifty shower caddy thing."

He chuckles and continues to hold his arm out to me. "Come on, Juno. One dance."

I accept his hand and rise off the blanket. His arms wrap around my waist, and I lock my hands behind his neck. We're so close, my nipples peak under the thin T-shirt I'm wearing. Since we're both in shorts, the hair on his legs rubs on my thighs as we circle around in one spot, our feet barely moving, but our emotions swirling like a tornado building momentum.

Tears build in my eyes and I lay my head on his chest, trying to commit the sound of his heartbeat to memory. I can't remember a day when we haven't seen one another, other than when his family goes on vacation.

His arms tighten around me and his chin rests on the top of my head. "I'm going to miss you so much."

I slide my arms from his neck to around his middle, hugging him. "I'm going to miss you too."

We've conveyed this string of words to one another before. It's no surprise to either of us, but maybe it's the slow song or the fact we're hugging tighter than I've ever hugged him before, but the words hold more weight and emotion this time around. A single tear rolls down my cheek.

The song comes to an end and "Firework" by Katy Perry plays. He loosens his arms.

I rest my chin on his chest, staring up at him. "I have one more gift for you."

He runs his thumb along my cheek, wiping away my tear. "This is plenty."

"It's kind of big."

His eyes search mine for some hint as to what it could be, but he'll never guess. And I know it's going to take some convincing. He won't go along with this right away.

"What is it?" he asks.

I break away from his hold and go to my bag, where I pull out a condom. "I want you to take my virginity."

The shadows from the lanterns mask me from seeing exactly what he's thinking.

"Why?"

"Because we're going to college, and sooner or later, I'm going to want to cross that off my list. I don't want to be a virgin forever." It sounds crazy as the words spill from my mouth, but Emily's words from when I was thirteen and hadn't had my first kiss yet ring in my ears. Colton is the one I want to remember my first time being with.

"That's not a reason, Juno." He rushes by me, sits on the bench, and puts his hands in his hair. "You can't just use me to get rid of your virginity. That's not how it's supposed to work."

I sit next to him on the bench. Close, but far enough that we don't touch. My hands press between my thighs and I lean forward. "I'm not using you. I don't want to remember my first time as something bad or something I regret. I'd never regret it if it's you."

He turns his head to face me. "This is huge. This isn't asking to borrow my bike while I'm gone. Or me leaving my lucky rabbit's foot."

"Do you still have that rabbit's foot?"

He chuckles at my ability to change the topic so quickly. "Be serious."

"I was. Do you?"

He shrugs. "I think it's in my dresser drawer or something." He buries his head back in his hands. "You do realize I'm a virgin too?"

I had my suspicions but didn't know for sure. His ex-girlfriend Monica was clear nothing had happened between them and told me it was my fault. That I play mind games and the two of us get off on pretending we're only friends.

"I didn't know for sure, but..." I slide along the bench, so we're hip to hip. "That's kind of perfect, right? We both lose our virginity to one another. That way we're ready for when we want to have sex. You're my best friend, and I trust you so much. I trust you to be gentle and understanding. I really want my first to be you."

He bites his lip. "Only you would come up with this plan."

"I'm sure we aren't the only best friends to lose their virginity to each other."

He sits up straight and his cheeks fill with air that he slowly releases. "On one condition."

I turn to face him, propping my one leg up on the bench. "What?"

"We kiss and have some foreplay. I'm not just gonna put the condom on and slide in."

My body zings with electricity that he wants some intimacy with his sex. But I'm not surprised. That's Colton. "You think I'm going to complain about kissing?"

"It's going to be weird." A groan rumbles up his throat. "Will this change things with us?"

I take his hand and lock it between mine. "No. We always know our friendship is the most important thing."

He nods again and rocks back, entwining our fingers together. Sitting up, his eyes flare to mine and his free hand rises and cups my cheek. "Juno, you're my everything. I cannot lose you, so I'm trusting you that you can handle any feelings that happen afterward."

I blanch. "It's me. Of course I can handle my feelings."

A smirk crosses his lips and he leans forward, placing his lips on mine. It takes us a moment to get comfortable, but once he slides his tongue along my lips, I'm shifting forward and releasing our clasped hands so I can touch him.

Before I can straddle him, he draws the kiss to a close and leads me to the blanket. Colton lays me down and his lips land on mine once again. Our tongues glide together sloppily, but I enjoy every second. His fingers graze down my body, his hand sliding up the hem of my shirt, goose bumps chasing the feel of his hand on my breast.

He leans back to ask, "Is this okay?"

I nod, and his lips trail across my neck. He lifts my T-shirt and unclasps my bra with a perfection that has me thinking he practiced this move at some point. As his mouth closes over my nipple, I arch off the blanket, wanting and needing more from him. This is nothing like prom night when I let Pete feel me up over my dress while we made out. The energy coursing through my entire body feels as if my hand is on one of those electronic balls at the science center that make your hair stand up.

I bring his face up to mine, my hands sliding under his shirt because I want to feel his skin and the chest he's teased me with all summer when he's been swimming in his board shorts.

His heavy breathing sends shivers up my spine as his face lands in the crook of my neck and we dry hump with most of our clothes still on. His hard length makes me widen my legs to get more friction on my sensitive area.

"I think I'm ready. Are you ready?" I say.

He nods and we both strip ourselves. I lie on the blanket, the moonlight falling over his body allowing me to see his shaking hands sliding the condom down his length. I've never seen a penis besides my brothers' and that was obviously way different than this. For a moment, I second-guess that this is what we should do.

But then Colton's body weight presses down on me and it feels right, and his knees widen my legs farther. The tip of his penis pushes at my opening.

"I'm going to take this slow, okay?"

I nod. He pushes in slightly, I wince, and he withdraws. "Maybe this is a bad idea. I don't want to hurt you."

My hands grip his shoulders. "No, please. I'm good." I kiss the hollow of his neck, which relaxes him.

His head falls into my neck again and I hold his body on top of mine as I close my eyes, breathing heavily through the pain.

"Shit, Juno. I'm not sure."

"Fast. Just do it fast, Colt." My hands grip his shoulders.

He sighs in my ear and pulls back his hips. "I love you, Juno."

Those four words shift my attention from the pain. It isn't until he's already completely inside me and the pain hits and subsides slightly that I'm back in the moment.

I'm sure he meant he loves me as a friend, and I love him too.

He moves inside me, the two of us awkwardly trying to get into a rhythm that just doesn't seem to come.

"I'm sorry. Can you stop moving for a second." Colton laughs and thrusts inside me, but he's being gentle because he's worried that he's going to hurt me.

For a moment, we're on the same page and his thrusts and his breathing increase. I love hearing how much he's enjoying this.

"I can't go much longer," he says like a warning.

My mind is in so many places, I'm positive I'm not going to orgasm. I heard most girls don't their first time anyway.

"Go ahead, Colt," I say.

"Not until you," he pants.

"Don't worry about it."

My name comes out of his mouth right before he stills inside me. "I'm sorry."

I run my hands through his hair and stare at his face only millimeters from mine. I take my last opportunity to kiss him, and his body falls on me as his tongue explores my mouth.

We lie on that blanket for the entire night. We don't have sex again, but we do kiss, and when dawn arrives, Colton leaves for college.

Colton was right to worry. That night changed us forever.

FOURTEEN

Colton

I knock on Brigette's apartment door. The playlist I made her of my favorite songs is playing inside.

She opens the door. Her hair is pulled into a high bun, and she's dressed in yoga pants and a short T-shirt that shows her stomach.

"Colton? What are you doing here?" She's surprised to find me here because I never called.

It's about time we talk everything out. She's been dodging me, and the fact she doesn't kiss me on the cheek says I was right that she's worried.

"Can I come in?"

She steps out of the doorway and grabs her phone from the waist of her yoga pants, turning off the music coming through the speaker. Coming here always feels weird because the setup is the same as Brooklyn's apartment was when she lived in this complex.

"I'm just cleaning so after the wedding, we can move it all out and I can get my security deposit back." She goes to the fridge. "Drink?"

"No. I'm good." I sit on her couch.

Her furniture is sparse because she doesn't have a ton of money. She's still working under Dr. Murphy and me because she's recently graduated. Still, there's enough room for her next to me. However, she grabs a sparkling water and sits on the floor across from me, crossing her legs and sipping her drink. I guess this is how it's going to be.

"I should have told you about Juno."

"That you love her, you mean?" she asks, eyebrows raised.

"No. I mean, I love her, yeah. She's my best friend." Which is all true. All these feelings coming to the surface have to be because of Juno trying to kiss me the night of the triple baby shower. That my subconscious is saying, "You finally have a chance at her, take it."

"Is that all?" she asks.

I look at the carpeted floor, thinking about Brooklyn's wedding and how she ended up finding Wyatt right after she was left at the altar. How happy they are now with their new baby.

"You're going to have to trust me on the Juno thing, okay? We've been friends a long time and I think me getting married is just changing things. It's weird for both of us." I'm being as honest as I can, but Brigette's slight scowl suggests she wants to dig more.

Our past is our past, in all truth. I don't go prying into hers, so she shouldn't pry into mine. What difference does it make?

"I have something I really need to talk to you about," I

say. "Dr. Murphy is going to call you into his office after the wedding."

She sits up straighter, wrapping her arms around her legs. "Dr. Murphy? Why?"

"I mentioned to you how I want to eventually take over the practice once he retires? I want to buy him out and make Four Paws my own. He was on board before, but now he feels me marrying you changes things. I need you to reassure him it won't."

"Okay. What is he going to ask me?"

"He's going to ask you if you see your life here in Lake Starlight."

Her head falls back, and she winds it around as if her neck hurts. "I thought I'd be okay with that, but now with the Juno thing, it feels weird."

"You have nothing to worry about."

I know she hears the aggravation in my tone because she narrows her eyes at me. "You know." She stands, placing her sparkling water on the table. "I never did ask you why you agreed to this arrangement."

I should've known she wouldn't let the Juno thing go. I'm not sure if she's just too proud or if she's worried that I won't honor my commitment.

She picks up a rag and dusts the bookcase behind her, picking up knickknacks and picture frames that really should be packed up.

"I'm doing it as a favor to you because you asked." I'm positive I told her that, but even so, the paperwork in the folder I'm holding feels as if it weighs about a thousand pounds right now.

"Really? Because I kind of wonder if you're not doing it to get Juno jealous."

I place the folder on the table and stand, needing to

exert some energy by pacing before I tell her again that my relationship with Juno is none of her business.

Sure, maybe making Juno jealous is part of it, but I won't tell Brigette that. At first, I was so pissed with Juno when Brigette asked me if I would want to marry her that I agreed on impulse. Then once the reality of what it would mean set in, proposing to Brigette seemed like a good way to force myself to get on with my life. Get over the one woman it seems I can never have. I've grown tired of pining away after something that's never going to happen. I needed *something* more than just my willpower to snap me out of it. This seemed like it would do the trick.

"I'm doing this as a favor to you, so now I'm asking you, as a favor to me, to tell Dr. Murphy that you see your future here in Lake Starlight."

"I'm not sure I feel comfortable now."

"Then no marriage. No green card."

She whips around. "I trust you with so much, why wouldn't you tell me about her?"

This entire town thinks I'm madly in love with Juno—and they're right. I am. But Juno's not in love with me and I'm done with the pitying looks. I tried to push her out of her comfort zone. Tried to assure her I'd never leave her again like I did when I left for college. But she doesn't believe we're worth the risk.

Then again, maybe I'm mad because I rashly went into this decision with Brigette. I was upset, and that's why I asked Juno to match me with someone. I didn't know Brigette was trying to be matched with someone in the hopes of getting her green card since her student visa would be ending. Neither did Juno. She thought Brigette was a twenty-something looking for love.

"I didn't think it was need-to-know information. I don't

know anything about you other than what I have to. Questions we'll be asked, that's the information we know about one another. Our favorites, our family, our friends."

"And Juno is your friend." She raises her arms to dust the top shelf of the bookcase and I spot a bandage under her left breast on her upper ribcage.

"Did you hurt yourself?"

She looks down, falls back to her heels, and the guilty look on her face says there's more to that bandage. "I got a tattoo."

"Where at?"

"There's only one tattoo parlor in this small town. Where do you think?"

"By whom?" Because I think I already know by whom—the man who keeps bringing in his new puppy for stupid reasons.

"Rhys," she says with a shrug.

"So maybe I'm not the only one who has eyes for someone else."

"Do you honestly think I would jeopardize this for a fling?" She puts her hands on her hips and squares her eyes on me.

She has much more to lose, except I really don't want to go to jail for this. After I made the decision and filed the first round of paperwork, I figured a three year commitment to her wasn't anything I couldn't handle. It'd give me plenty of time to force myself to get some distance from Juno and get over her, move on with my life and accept that Juno would not play a romantic role in it.

My phone dings in my pocket, but I ignore it.

"I have the prenup." I pick up the folder. "I had my lawyer put a clause in there about Four Paws should Dr. Murphy sell it to me. I'll own that by myself, and we'll each leave this marriage with what we had coming into it."

She nods. We were clear that when this is over, we go our separate ways, but I wanted a fail-safe just in case.

When she disappears into the kitchen, I open the folder and see our names there on the paperwork. Sometimes I wonder how I got myself into this position. But there's no sense looking back. I'm in it and I'm a man of my word, so regardless, I'll be marrying Brigette next week.

She returns with a pen and scrolls her name across the lines that are flagged for her signature.

I close the folder and leave her apartment, pulling my phone out of my pocket.

Dori Bailey: *I need your help. I'm at a bar in Anchorage and Ethel drank too much. Pick us up?*

This has to be a joke. Why would Dori be in Anchorage? Plus, I've never seen Ethel drink more than a single glass of wine without complaining about heartburn. But regardless, it seems I'll be driving to Anchorage.

Me: *Sure. Just send me the address.*

My phone pings with the address of the bar. Great.

I OPEN the door of Tipsy Turvy, which sounds like somewhere Dori would go to. As soon as my eyes adjust from the sun to darkness, I spot Juno standing there talking to a bartender.

"Colton?" she asks, her forehead scrunched up.

"Did Dori call you too? I wish she'd told me before I drove all the way out here."

"No. She's in the back though." Juno rolls her eyes, finishes talking to the bartender, and ushers me to the back. "Kingston's big mouth told her I was doing this blind speed dating thing here tonight, and she said she wanted to come. Thought that I needed her and Ethel in case some older men showed up."

"She told me Ethel was drunk and she needed a ride home?"

Juno scoffs. "Neither one of them has had one drink and *I* drove them here. Unfortunately."

I stop her before we go through a door to the back room. "We should talk."

She's shaking her head before I get a chance to continue. "Later, okay? I'm so nervous about tonight and I just need to concentrate on that right now."

I can't fault her for not wanting to hash out our history when she's working.

"Maybe we can ride back to Lake Starlight together. Ethel could drive your car?"

"Um... no, but we could meet up later tonight if you want."

"Perfect."

We walk through the door, and lo and behold, Dori and Ethel are at a table, playing cards.

"Grandma, did you tell Colton to come here?"

"Did I?" She looks at Ethel.

I raise my phone in my hand. "I have the text."

"Oh yes, funny, I thought I was messaging Kingston. You know how he works in Anchorage. Thought he'd be on his way home."

"I told you Kingston was coming tonight." Juno

straightens chairs and tables that are lined up with partitions like voting booths. Even when they switch seats, they won't be able to see one another.

"Oh, did you? My memory must be going." Dori taps her temple. "It's not so good anymore."

"I'm the matchmaker. Colton is getting married, remember?" Juno's voice has an edge to it I've never heard directed toward Dori.

"You are not too old for me to take you over my knee, Juno." Dori's stern voice says she's serious.

"I would have helped you with all this anyway." I straighten some of the partitions. "This is ingenious. Where did you get the idea from?"

"Kingston. Go figure, but it's pretty cool, I think. It's a bit of a twist. Hopefully, it will pull some people in."

"Definitely."

A waitress comes into the room and asks if we need anything, so I order a beer. She nods and walks away.

"Anyone else coming besides Kingston?"

Juno bends over to retrieve something from her bag and her ass is in my face. Her ass has been in my face plenty of times, but this time it's a struggle not to grab her by her hips and pull her into me.

I have a lot of guilt for not telling Juno why I'm marrying Brigette, but I can't chance it getting out. No one but Brigette and myself knows this is a green-card-only kind of marriage, and if something leaked, I could be in some serious trouble.

The waitress returns and places my beer on the table. "You have some women who just came in. Micah is getting them a drink, then they're on their way back."

"Great." Juno's eyes get all wide and excited like they do when something she's been anticipating finally arrives.

"Kingston and some of his firefighter buddies are coming tonight too. So at least I'm offering some good-looking guys."

I haven't asked her why she's doing this. She's always done strictly matchmaking with a personal touch. But I'm not going to ask her right now in front of everyone.

"Rummy!" Ethel screams and puts her cards on the table.

Dori scowls and tosses her cards on the table. "I gotta pee."

Dori stands and leaves for the bathroom, Ethel following as if their bladders are in sync.

A woman pops her head into the room. "Is this where we're supposed to be?"

Juno rushes over. "Yes. Yes. Come—" She abruptly stops speaking, making me look over. "Stella?"

"Kingston's Stella?" I whisper more to myself as Juno looks over at me.

But it's Stella who looks as if she might faint.

FIFTEEN

Juno

Holy shit, as if Colton showing up wasn't enough of a surprise, Stella Harrison is here.

In Alaska.

In Anchorage.

Not in New York.

"Stella?" I say.

She catches her drink before it falls. "Juno?" Her eyes scan the room. "Colton?"

The last time we saw Stella was at Holly and Austin's wedding, which seems like ages ago. She and Kingston talked the majority of the night, but after that, nothing that I know of. If he knows she's back in town, he hasn't shared it with me.

"Oh, um, you're running this?" Stella says. "My friend from work thought it'd be fun."

She's been here long enough to have friends at work?

Dori and Ethel's arguing rings out of the hallway as they come out of the bathroom.

My eyes widen. "Oh my God, hide."

Her friend's attention darts between Stella and me as though she's asking, "Is this chick serious?" But Stella must hear it in my voice because she disappears behind the partitions and hides in one of the booths I've set up.

"Oh, someone showed up." Grandma Dori beams as though she's surprised.

Thanks for the encouragement, *Grandma*.

"Colton's going to drive you home now." My eyes widen at Colton, who's sipping his beer.

"He's drinking. I told my son I never drive with someone who's been drinking," Ethel says.

Colton stares at his beer. "I've had about two sips."

"Drinking is drinking. I don't know your tolerance. Maybe it's zero. I'll drive us." Ethel puts her hand out to Colton for his keys.

He stares at her hand then lifts his gaze to me with an expression that suggests I would never make him do such a thing as drive all the way back to Lake Starlight with Ethel behind the wheel of his truck. But I know Grandma, and if she sees Stella here, all hell is gonna break loose. Rumors will spread, and if Stella's been hiding out in Anchorage, she's not ready to face what happened all those years ago.

I always felt close to Stella, what with her only being a few years younger than me. When the guys wanted to start a band, she'd hang around the garage, and she was my bleacher buddy during the baseball games.

"Just let her drive," I plead.

"And your name is?" Dori asks Stella's friend.

"Cami."

"Well, Cami, this is Juno. She's my granddaughter and a real matchmaker. It's been in her mother's blood for generations, so you should trust her with who you should be matched with tonight."

"Grandma, it's a speed dating thing." I kiss Grandma Dori on the cheek with the hopes it gets her out of here.

Colton is still sipping his beer.

"You took another sip," Ethel says like a sibling who wants to get their other sibling in trouble.

"Just let her drive?" I say to him, trying to pull him to the door.

"But my truck?" he says as if I'm crazy.

I probably am, but I really need to get Dori out of here and tell Stella to leave before Kingston shows up, otherwise, my entire blind speeding date thing is gonna be a bust and I'm never going to be able to pay my bills. "What harm can it do?"

"Are you seriously asking me that right now?" Colton says.

"I need Dori out," I whisper.

She's busy naming off my qualifications to Cami, Stella's friend.

"I get it, but it's my truck, Juno."

Ethel watches like a hawk to see if Colton has another sip of beer. I know that the only way they're leaving is if Colton gives her the keys. Eventually, Colton realizes it too.

"You so owe me for this, and I mean huge." Colton stands, downs the rest of his beer, but right before Ethel is about to say something, he drops the keys in her hand. "Bigger than that time you accidentally kneed me in the nuts when we were wrestling."

I giggle, remembering how his face turned blue. I felt so bad. I hope he can still have children. I rise up on my tiptoes and kiss his cheek. "I owe you big. Promise. Name it and I'll deliver."

He wraps his arm around my waist and turns his face to me. We're millimeters apart and my heart pounds.

"No take-backs," he says.

"No take-backs. I promise."

Then he kisses my cheek and releases me. Now I'm not so sure I want him to go.

"Let's go, Golden Girls," Colton says. "We will be driving five over the speed limit."

"I can't lose my license, Colton Stone," Ethel says.

He winks at me one more time before the three of them leave the room.

"It's safe now," I say to Stella, who peeks up over the partition.

"Thank you. I do not want to be in Buzz Wheel again." Stella sips her drink that's halfway gone now. "So are you and Colton finally together?"

I shake my head. "No, he's actually getting married next week."

Her eyes widen. "Really?" She looks at her friend. "They were, like, the best friends you always thought would get married."

"You're one to talk. What about my brother?"

Her friend sips her wine. "Do tell? Stella's like a vault. I've yet to figure out the combination to get her to talk about her life."

Stella sips her drink and her eyes plead for me not to say anything.

My head rears back when I remember who else is

supposed to be here tonight. "I forgot! Kingston and his firefighter buddies are coming tonight."

This time the drink does fall from Stella's hands. There's no time to react because I hear a gaggle of men walking down the hall. I'm guessing they're firefighter because they're loud and boisterous, razzing one another about something.

"Um. Just stay here," I say.

This is not what I had planned when I came here.

Walking out the door of our private room, I shut it behind me and see one of Kingston's buddies who's been to the apartment a few times.

"Juno." Lou hugs me so my feet lift off the floor. "Kingston said we had to come tonight. Plus, you know I like the ladies." He sets me back down and winks. "This here is Cory, Shawn, and Jorge."

I say hello to them all. "Where's Kingston?"

"Oh. He's running late and then there's the paperwork, so I wouldn't expect him."

Just as Lou tells me, my phone dings. I pull it out to see it from Kingston.

Kingston: *Sorry, I can't make it tonight. Next time, I swear. But I sent some guys over for you. ;)*

I can't be upset with him. Work is work and he's done more than enough already by arranging this room. The anxiety squeezing my body eases a little.

"Well, boys, just give me a minute to get all the ladies set up." I smile and rush back into the private room, shooting Stella a look to say no worries.

After I get all the women situated at their tables behind

the cardboard partitions, I pop my head back in the hallway. "Come on in." I open the door for them, and they file in.

A few more people come through the door and I position everyone in a seat.

After the speed dating is over, some couples go into the other bar area to continue their conversations. I'm packing up my stuff when Stella approaches me.

"Hey, it was a great event."

"You didn't find anyone, right? My brother might kill me."

We both giggle nervously. Kingston's always an awkward conversational topic between us.

"About him," she says. "I don't want to put you in this position, but could you keep it to yourself that you saw me here? I mean, I'm not ready to see him just yet."

"Sure." I hate that I'm keeping a secret from Kingston, but he's better off not knowing until I'm sure Stella can deal with the ramifications of seeing my brother.

"Thank you. I promise I'll come out from the shadows eventually. I wasn't really planning on coming home at all, but..."

I stop putting paperwork in my bag. "Are you okay?"

She sighs, looking crestfallen. "I don't want to burden you with yet another secret, but it's hard being back and not telling anyone. It's like I'm alone on an iceberg in the middle of the ocean. Cami's great, but we haven't really gotten to the 'call me if you're in jail and I'll bail you out, no questions asked' stage yet."

"What's going on?"

"My mom is sick and she's being stubborn, saying that she doesn't need my help. So I moved to Anchorage to be closer, but not too close, for reasons you must understand.

But you're telling me that Kingston works for the Anchorage Fire Department?"

I nod. "Yeah, but he'll likely be mostly smoke jumping soon. He'll be gone more than he's home."

"Okay. Again, I'm sorry. You won't have to keep my secret forever. One day I have to face Kingston and deal with everything and put it behind me for good. We chatted at Austin's wedding, but it wasn't about anything of consequence. I know the day is coming when I'll have to deal with what happened, but at the same time, I can't imagine putting your brother permanently in my rearview mirror, you know?"

I offer her a small smile that I hope conveys how sorry I feel for her. Grabbing a pen and paper, I scribble down my number. "Call me if you need to talk."

She puts it in her purse. "Thank you. Do you want to talk about Colton getting married?"

That's like opening one of those cans of slinky snakes and a million silky fabric-covered coils flying up in your face. Then again, I can't really talk to my sisters, because I know what their advice will be. Break up his engagement. But Stella understands how horrible it is to love a man enough to want his happiness over your own. It's the reason she disappeared all those years ago.

Still, I feel like a boat lost at sea and all these lighthouses are shining to guide me to shore, but I have no idea which way is the best way to go. Who's to say I won't end up following the wrong light and end up on an island all by myself?

"No. Not yet."

Her hand covers mine and she smiles as though she's saying touché. "I get it, but at some point, you have to face that you'll no longer be the first woman in his life. Are you ready for that?"

I shrug.

She squeezes my hand again before stealing the pen and writing her number on a napkin. "You can call me anytime."

We say goodbye and I get in my car, hammering a text to Colton to ask if it's okay that I come over. Brigette could be over there. He tells me he's up and to come right over.

Here goes nothing.

Colton

I answer the door to find Juno standing on the porch. Usually she slides past me with a brief hello and a long story of what just happened to her because something weird always happens to Juno. I figured she'd be talking nonstop about Stella's reappearance before I opened the door all the way. But she's just silent and stands there.

"Do you want to come in?" I ask, stepping to the side.

She looks me over. "Are you alone?" She clears her throat. "I mean, is Brigette here?"

I narrow my eyes. "No."

"Phew. Okay." Now she slides by me. "I realized when I knocked that I can't just barge in anymore. I'll have to ring the bell so I don't interrupt the newlyweds."

I shut the front door and ignore the squeeze of my heart at her comment. "How was the speed dating thing?"

She shrugs, burying her head in my fridge. "It was okay

but made a decent amount of money. I feel like I should pay Kingston a portion. Almost every guy there was a first responder of some kind."

"And Stella?" I ask, sitting on my breakfast stool and watching her pick up takeout boxes to smell the contents.

She peeks out of the fridge. "She wants me to keep it a secret that I saw her." She clenches her jaw in an 'eek' expression. Juno and secrets don't always mix. "She's not ready to see him."

She shuts the fridge and opens an orange chicken container from Wok For U, moving over to my silverware drawer to grab a fork.

"Want me to heat it up for you?"

She waves me off. "I just need to eat something fast. My stomach is crazy right now and I think if I eat, I might not throw up." A piece of chicken rests in front of her lips. "How was your ride? Truck okay?" Then she puts the piece of chicken in her mouth and chews.

"Thankfully, yes." I steal the fork from her container, pierce my own piece of cold chicken, and eat it. "My truck is now parked in the garage, but Ethel demanded they drop me off first and take my truck with them. I ended up calling Duke Thompson to drive them back home."

"She's just being cautious," she says.

"I took one for the team. What do I get in return?"

She laughs, but it's her nervous laugh. Something's up with her. She only eats for fear of throwing up when she has to tell someone something she doesn't want to. Like the time she had to tell Savannah she scratched her car when she borrowed it. Or when she told me that she did go home with Trey. She ate an entire container of fried rice before finally admitting that to me.

"What's up, Juno?"

She looks up with those doe eyes as though I'm a hunter with an arrow pointed at her. "Why do you think something's up?" she mumbles around her food.

I say nothing but give her the look.

She takes the fork from me and places it in the sink, packages up the orange chicken, and puts it away. Hopefully, whatever it is isn't a big deal. Because when she tells me whatever it is she has to, I want to tell her that I understand this whole situation is weird and uncomfortable, but we'll eventually get back on track. Even if it's three years from now when I divorce Brigette.

Grabbing a water, she unscrews the top then gulps down half the bottle like she just finished working out. She puts the water down and her gaze falls to the counter. "Can we not talk about big things, your wedding included, tonight? I kind of miss us and want to just chill."

My shoulders fall. She's right. We haven't hung out in a long time. Like since before I announced the engagement. Maybe all this craziness with us is because we miss one another. "Definitely. Want to binge something?"

She smiles and rounds the counter toward my family room. "Yeah. I'd love that." She grabs the remote and turns on my television, scrolling through Netflix. "What has Colton been watching lately?" She presses on my name instead of hers because yes, we share a Netflix account. "Documentary city. You need some comedy in your life."

I join her on the couch, stretching my legs on the ottoman between us. She does the same but on the opposite side of the couch. We've done this millions of times. Sometimes she's even fallen asleep with her head in my lap. One time when I fell during a soccer game, she made me stay up all night to make sure I didn't have a concussion. I woke up the next morning and we were somehow entangled together. Her head on my stomach and my arm around her back, my boner straining my track pants. She didn't let me live that one down for years.

"How about this?" The yellow box on the screen is around a chick flick. "It's supposed to be funny."

"Fine." I don't have the heart to argue with her because I'm just happy she's here. "Just so we're clear, that's two you owe me now." I hold up two fingers.

She laughs, clicking on the button. "Okay, after this movie, I'll watch two of your boring documentaries."

She leans back, and I stand and turn off the lights so we can watch in darkness.

Fifteen minutes into the classic rom-com movie where two people hate one another but are secretly in love, Juno pauses the movie. "Did you see that popcorn? Let's make some."

"I need to find a movie where they don't eat," I say.

She stands from the couch. "You love recreating the food from movies."

"Eh."

"What about that time we made the sandwich from *Spanglish*? I didn't hear any complaints then." She's got me, but I never would've made the sandwich if she wasn't rewinding the movie and watching it fifty times over.

"The tiramisu from *No Reservations* was a pain in the ass."

She grabs the microwave popcorn from my cabinet and takes it out of the plastic bag. I love how comfortable we are in each other's space. "Yeah, we'll leave that to Rome now."

We both laugh.

She punches the buttons on my microwave and slides up on the counter. "It's not going to be the same. We should buy a popcorn maker if we want it to look like that."

"That's stretching it kind of far." I pull out chocolate chips and drop them on the counter. Her eyes light up. "What about the *Pulp Fiction* cheeseburger?"

That might've been the best thing ever.

Her head falls back. "Ah, don't remind me because I'm going to drag you to the grocery store right now to buy the ingredients."

"I wouldn't be opposed."

"Tell me, Mr. I Don't Like to Recreate Foods from Movies, which would you choose, the cheeseburger from *Pulp Fiction* or the huevos rancheros from *Wolf of Wall Street*?"

I grab a bowl and put it in Juno's lap before taking the popcorn out of the microwave and shaking it into the bowl. "That's a hard one. I guess as long as the food doesn't talk, I'll take any of the meals."

She kicks me in the thigh and I back away, laughing. When we were nine, we watched *Shrek* and Juno refused to eat gingerbread men or women. She even put a tray of them that her mom made on the back porch to be set free.

"It's not funny." She hops down from the counter and stares at the bowl of popcorn. "This isn't going to cut it."

I shake my head, already knowing Juno well enough to know she won't be satisfied until she gets her fix. Grabbing my keys off the counter, I jiggle them in my hand. "What are we going for?"

She bites her lip and her classic smirk emerges.

"*The Chef*'s pasta?" I ask.

She nods.

"At least you chose something fairly easy."

We file into my truck and I back out, past her car, onto the street. She fiddles with the radio.

"Hold up, turn that back," I say, and she does.

"Oh, I like this one too." She relaxes back in the seat.

As "Get to You" by Michael Ray plays on the radio, we drive through the dark streets of Lake Starlight to the town's outskirts, where there's one grocery store open until midnight. I'm surprised Juno likes this song because the lyrics sound a lot like her. Although she's lived her life in Lake Starlight, she runs away from any sort of commitment or emotions. Sometimes I wish it were as easy as taking a pin to pop her bubble to make her realize what she's missing out on.

"Are you even gonna be hungry once we get home?" I ask as we climb out of the truck and enter the desolate grocery store.

She grabs a cart and pushes it, riding it until it stops right before it runs into a bin of potatoes. "When am I not hungry?" She steers the cart to the greens area to find the parsley. "What else do we need?"

"Just the pasta and fresh garlic. I have everything else." I grab three bulbs of garlic.

She diverts to the bakery section, picking up a pack of cookies.

Midway through aisles we don't need to be looking at, I pick up a ball that's on a display and throw it at her ass, but she doesn't retaliate. She barely even reacts.

"What's the matter?" I lean in close after putting the ball back in the rack.

She shrugs and I follow her line of vision to the flower department.

"What flowers did you guys pick out?" she asks.

"I thought we weren't talking about the wedding?" I can't even answer her because Brigette did that by herself.

"Things are going to change. This might be our last time making food from movies. I mean, I guess we could do it with her." The tone in her voice says that's not really an option.

I desperately want to tell Juno the truth, so she knows not much has to change. I mean, Brigette will be living with me, but we're not a *real* couple. Juno wouldn't be the third wheel. But if I tell Juno, I'm putting myself and Brigette at risk. Not that I think Juno would tell anyone, but sometimes secrets slip. This one is better off staying between the people who have the most to lose if it comes out.

"Nothing is going to change," I say.

She huffs. Yeah, I don't believe me either.

"Come on. Let's enjoy tonight. Remember?" I knock her shoulder with mine.

She nods. "It's just hard. You're right. I was stupid to think we'd just be best friends until we grew old."

I can't do this anymore. I have to tell her. I place my hand on hers. "Juno."

Her eyes meet mine, and they look so sad. I'm definitely making the right decision. "What?"

"Surprise!" Rome jumps out in front of our cart. "What are you two crazy kids doing at the grocery store this late?"

We look in his arms to find Little Debbie brownies, a carton of ice cream, and three of the balls I just threw at Juno.

"More like what are you doing?" Juno asks. "Harley having cravings?"

He nods. "Yeah, and it has to be the Little Debbie's with the walnuts on top, not the candy things. But the kids like the candy ones, so I have to buy both. And I'm trying not to be offended that she never craves what I can make her. I mean, shouldn't that be the benefit of being married to a chef?"

Juno laughs because we know how Rome is about his

cooking. Calista and Dion still like the instant mac n' cheese over his authentic homemade version. "Well, you can make brownies for me."

Rome looks in our cart. "What are you guys making? Spaghetti, garlic, and parsley?"

"Ever seen *The Chef*? We're making the pasta from it."

Rome pulls out his phone and searches for the clip on YouTube then stares at us. "Is this what gets you guys all hot?"

Juno slaps him on the arm. "Rome!"

"I'm offended you didn't come to me. I can cook this a helluva lot better than the two of you." He dumps his things into our cart. "Come on. Harley will love it too. We'll get more. I'm cooking tonight."

We share a look behind his back.

"Isn't it late?" Juno asks.

"I'm a chef. I'm used to being up late. Plus, Harley has insomnia with this pregnancy. She'll appreciate the company."

Before I can argue, we're leaving the grocery store and heading to Rome's house. So much for my last night with Juno.

SEVENTEEN

Juno

The day has come. The day I lose my best friend.

Dodging Colton until his wedding day was easier than I thought. He only stopped by my office once, and I ventured out of my way to never pass Four Paws, even convincing Calista to go to a park farther away so he wouldn't see me outside. Brigette hasn't messaged me, so she must have decided the double dating thing isn't a good idea.

After checking with Brigette to make sure it was okay to bring Jason, he agreed to be my date for the wedding, but I think after tonight, I'll tell him we're probably better off as friends. The spark just isn't there. If I'm lucky, he'll still hire me to find someone for him.

We walk the path next to Cozy Cottage B&B and I spot Harley talking with the owner, Selene, by the back door, the kids hovering around. Rome is catering the event, so he's busy under a great big white tent, telling servers to be ready because the meal will come right after the ceremony.

The path along Selene's garden is beautiful with spring in full bloom. The flowers aren't overgrown, some looking like new buds just now coming to life. The bridal arch is decorated with an array of peach and pastel flowers with limited greenery. There are a few short rows of white chairs. With Brigette's family not coming, they kept the ceremony small.

"It's beautiful," I softly say to myself. I expected nothing less. Brigette's taste is exquisite.

There are no ushers, but halfway down the aisle, Mrs. Stone spots me and makes her way over.

"Juno," she says, taking my hands. Her gaze shifts to Jason and back to me. "Come check on the groom with me?"

"Um." I look at Jason, but he just smiles. "Jason, this is Colton's mom, Mrs. Stone."

"Macy." She holds out her hand. "This girl was supposed to be my daughter-in-law and I still can't get her to call me Macy."

Jason's eyebrows rise to his hairline and I don't blame him.

"Mrs. Stone, I was never going to marry Colton," I whisper.

She pats my hand. "Oh, you know what I mean. You were always so close, people assumed. I hoped." She puts her hand over her heart.

Great. This is the last thing I need to get through today.

"Come. You don't mind, do you, Jason? We'll only be a moment."

Mrs. Stone should team up with Grandma Dori. They'd be a power couple in getting people to go along with their agendas.

"Not at all. I'll save your seat," Jason says.

I smile graciously. "Thank you."

We walk back down the aisle the way I came, Austin and Holly watching me from the corner of their eyes. I see they didn't bring Easton.

"Juno." Harley stops to say hello right before we're about to walk into the house.

Selene starts talking to Mrs. Stone about how the bride's room and the groom's room are on opposite floors, that she put Colton in her painting room to make sure of it.

"Where are you going?" Harley whispers.

"Aunt Juno. Aunt Juno!" Dion jumps up and down in front of me, grabbing at my dress. I take his hands before he ruins it.

"Dion," Harley scolds and he stares up at me with a look like I got him in trouble.

"Mrs. Stone wants me to check on Colton." I give Harley the look that suggests I should not see him. It's bad enough I have to witness him getting married. I'd shut my eyes and plug my ears like a child during the ceremony if I could.

"Good luck," Harley says.

As I'm giving her a "yeah right" expression, Stella's head pop out of the stairway. What the hell?

"What's up, Dion?" Kingston rounds the corner.

Dion runs over to him. He's the fun uncle. Kingston picks him up and twirls him around. My little brother is in a suit and looks way too grown-up. When did he get so old and where is that little boy with the mop of brown hair who sulked in the corner all the time?

"Come on, I heard they have bubbles," he whispers to Calista and Phoebe at his legs.

All three cheer and follow him as if he's Santa Claus.

"Kingston, those are for after," Selene yells, hearing everything even if she's distracted by someone else.

"Only a few, Mrs. Harrison." He winks.

I turn back to see Selene smiling at him as if he's her own.

"Okay, let's go, Juno." Mrs. Stone takes my hand and we slide through the glass door.

I give Harley one last look that I hope asks her to pray for me, and she laughs.

As we walk through the living area, I almost knock down a trinket of I have no idea what. There're a lot of trinkets. Selene is an artist and I love her work, but there's so much in here, I'm afraid of breaking something.

"Juno," Stella whispers, showing her face one more time after Mrs. Stone has released my hand on her way to the painting room, where Colton is getting ready.

"I'm just going to run to the bathroom, Mrs. Stone. I'll be right behind you."

She stops and sulks. "Hurry up. You were my excuse to go in there. But I am his mom, so the hell with it. It's his big day."

After her own pep talk, Mrs. Stone knocks on the door then enters. I don't hear Colton say anything, so I take it as a good sign.

Stella grabs my arm and drags me up the stairs. Easy for her—she's in jeans and a T-shirt. I'm in a dress and heels. She doesn't stop until we're in her room, where she shuts the door, locks it.

"Stella?" I ask in a tone that I hope conveys my concern for her sanity.

"Kingston is here."

I nod. "Yeah, it's Colton's wedding."

She paces, her hands on her hips. "I told Mom no weddings this year. It's too much for her. So I show up today on my day off, thinking I'll help around the house, see if she has any guests I can help out with, and I find her in the garden with the tent people. I had no idea, and now I'm trapped up here unless I want Kingston to see me."

"Would it really be that bad if he did?"

She peeks out the curtain. Her room looks over the entire property and her shoulders slump when she must spot him. "Whose kids are those?"

"Rome's," I say without looking.

"Man, he works fast. My mom told me how his wife just showed up with a baby."

I nod. Their story is kind of remarkable.

"King looks so... old. A good old. A mature old. His hair is darker than I remember from the wedding." She keeps staring.

"I think you should go down and let him see you. Work through the fear."

She shuts the curtain quickly. "What about you? I see my words from the other night haven't spurred you into confessing your feelings for Colton yet." She joins me on her childhood bed with the pink comforter. Her walls are still lined with trophies and medals.

"I can't stop the wedding." I fixate on my hands in my lap.

"Spill," she says.

I tell her everything since she's been gone.

After I'm done splitting my chest open and letting my heart flop in front of her, she's quiet for a moment. "Juno, you have to tell him."

"What?" My head rears back.

"You cannot let him marry someone else. What are you thinking? You'll just sit back and watch him have babies and live the life you imagined for the two of you? Lake Starlight is way too small for that. You'll never survive." Her hand covers mine. "My mom always says love is scary because there are only two ways love ends, but Juno, you not admitting to loving him doesn't make the feelings disappear."

"I just keep thinking the more I see him with her, the more I'll make peace with the fact that he'll never be mine. I care enough about him to want him to be happy, even if it's not with me. Other times I doubt myself and question if this is just jealousy and not love."

She tilts her head with an incredulous expression. "You loved that boy well before he became a man. You want to know one of the things about Kingston that made me run?"

"I don't know. Do I?"

Her eyes well with unshed tears. "Besides just being in the middle of him and Owen, when he told me he was fore-going college to be a smoke jumper... it was like he wanted to live on the edge every day of his life. He's always doing risky things—you know that as well as I do. It felt like one day I'd lose him to some horrific accident because he didn't care if he lived or died. So to love Kingston was scary because I only saw one way it ends—and that's with him on that hill right next to your parents. Don't be like me and walk away and ruin what could have been. Live your life like your parents would've wanted you to. It's okay to be scared. Just push forward anyway."

Just when I think she's done, she continues. "You're not that thirteen-year-old girl anymore. If it goes badly, you're strong. You'll be able to pull yourself up off the ground and go on living. Watching him marry someone else without ever telling him your true feelings? That's just being a coward."

I close my eyes. "It would hurt his fiancée if I break up the marriage. She's a great woman. I don't want to see her heartbroken."

She sighs and her shoulders sag. "If Colton loves you like everyone believes he does, you're saving both of them from a loveless marriage. Everyone deserves to have a guy who looks at them like Colton looks at you."

"How does he look at me?"

"The same way you look at him—like all your happiness is wrapped up in the other one." She pats my hand again. "Go tell him before it's too late."

My heart catches in my throat as I stand. Stella is right. How can I let him marry someone else without admitting my feelings to him?

"Thanks." The urge to tell Colton my feelings sparks and ignites a fire inside me.

She hugs me. "You're welcome."

"You sure you don't want to see King yet?"

She shakes her head. "It's not our time yet."

"But doesn't that go against all the advice you just gave me?"

She giggles. "Everyone knows that those who can, do, and those who can't, teach. One day I'll have to face him, but not today."

I nod, hoping that if our friendship grows, maybe I can persuade her. If Kingston knew she was living in Anchorage, he'd probably bang down every door to find her. Then it occurs to me—maybe she doesn't love Kingston like he loves her and that's why she doesn't want to see him. The thought depresses me.

I pick up the hem of my dress and rush down the stairs to the painting room. As my fist connects with the door, I realize maybe Colton doesn't love me like I love him anymore.

EIGHTEEN

Colton

Another knock sounds on the door and I swing it open, hoping it's someone telling me it's time. The longer I sit in here, the more doubts seep in. My mom's impromptu visit—where she talked about Juno and how she always envisioned me marrying her—didn't help. What kind of mom does that to her son when he's minutes away from getting married?

My parents have only met Brigette three times. I usually show up by myself, lying about Brigette's whereabouts. If they were to add up all the excuses I tell them, I'd probably find out she delivers more puppies and kitties than Dr. Murphy and I combined.

I open the door to find Juno standing there. She's gorgeous with her hair pulled up high on her head and her makeup all done. My gaze falls to the contours of her neck and the swell of her breasts peeking out from the top of her dress, but it's her necklace that I fixate on.

I take the small jagged half heart in my hand. "You wore this?"

She stares down between us. "I felt like I needed the reminder."

I drop the half of a best friends necklace and dig in my pocket, pulling out the other half. Juno insisted we get these when they were the hot thing. I told her I'd never wear it, which I never do, but as I put on my cufflinks this morning, I saw the half heart in my drawer, slightly tarnished from being stored away for so long, and I felt like I needed the reminder too.

That we're best friends forever, regardless of this decision I made so hastily.

"Are those donuts?" She spots the tray behind me.

Selene left an entire pastry dish and juice selection for me. Since I've been stuck in this room with paint fumes for so long, I've eaten more than I should. Juno doesn't wait for me to answer though—she heads to the tray and picks up a glazed donut.

"Juno?" I ask because here we are again like she has something to tell me. "What's going on?"

She holds the donut at her side and our eyes lock. "I have something to tell you." She pushes the rest of the donut into her mouth and wipes her hands with a napkin.

"What's the matter?" I ask.

She gulps down some apple juice and stares at me for a long time. "You're so important to me. The most important person in my life. I love my family, I do, but you, Colton... there's nothing you don't know about me. You do way too much for me, you know that, right?"

I shrug. I like to do things for her. "You do things for me too."

"Eh," she says.

I chuckle. If we weighed them on a scale, I probably do more, but I don't keep track, and neither should she.

A tear slips from her eye. "I'm sorry."

I step forward, my hand cradling her cheek and my thumb brushing the tear away. I haven't seen her look at me like this since... actually never. "Whoa, why are you crying?"

"Because I pushed you away all these years. Maybe the timing just wasn't right for us or maybe I was too scared. But I think I've been stupid..."

"What? Did something happen?"

"I love you, Colton." Her eyes close, another two tears slipping down her cheeks.

"I love you too. Today is emotional. Are you getting your period?" I pull her in for a hug, but she shoves me in the chest.

"I am not getting my period."

"Sorry." I'm not sure why she's so upset. I've bought her tampons in the past. It's a regular conversation when she's crabby.

"I'm telling you I love you."

I nod. "I know."

"No, Colton. I looovvve you." Her eyes go wide, and her head leans forward. "I'm *in* love with you."

Shock hits me like a Mack truck and I stand speechless in front of her.

I can barely hold her gaze. She cannot be telling me what I've wanted to hear for years on the day of my wedding. "What do you mean?"

She throws her arms in the air. "Like I want to kiss you, I love you. I want forever with you."

I step back from her, letting my hands fall from her face. "So you're attracted to me?"

Our attraction is clear. We've crossed that line a couple times, the last time being over two years ago. Then she hid me in her room when her family ambushed her apartment because Denver showed up and thought he'd lost Cleo forever. Her hiding me was a glaring red light that Juno wasn't ready yet. So after the family left, I sneaked out and told her it was a mistake before she had a chance.

"I mean, yeah, I'm attracted to you, but it's more than that."

"I'm about to get married," I say softly. Half of me is overjoyed that she's admitting her feelings. The other half is angry that it took me marrying someone else for her to realize them.

"I know." She presses her palms into her eyes. "I'm sorry. But I was talking to Stella and she convinced me that I should be upfront with you. It all sounded so good, but now that I just told you and you're not overjoyed, hugging me and confessing your own feelings, I'm thinking this was a very, very bad idea. I should go." She slides between an easel and me.

"Juno, stop." I turn on my heels, and she's facing the door. "The marriage isn't real."

She slowly circles to face me, and she tilts her head, waiting for more to come out of my mouth.

"Brigette's student visa is expiring and she wants to stay in the United States."

Her mouth drops open and she's quiet for a second. "You don't love her?"

I shake my head. "I wanted to tell you. So bad. Especially that night of the baby shower when you kissed me. But we couldn't risk it. If anyone finds out, I could be arrested."

"Oh my God," she says.

"Say something more," I urge.

She sits on one of Selene's stools. "That's not like you. Why would you agree to this?"

It's a fair question and it deserves an honest answer. I'm half surprised she didn't throw a tray of paints at me for lying to her this entire time. "I agreed to it after you told me you slept with Trey."

She's uncharacteristically quiet as she spins on the stool, staring at the floor. "You agreed to marry someone because I slept with Trey?"

She stands and walks to the other end of the room, staring out the window. Jack and Frannie are talking with Liam and Savannah. Frannie's head is buried in the stroller in front of Savannah.

"Yes."

"Do you know how stupid that is?"

"Do you know how stupid I felt when you told me? I thought what happened after that one night when we were drunk, that maybe..."

She whips around, startled by my sharp tongue. "No. I suppose I don't but—I—"

Years of built-up aggression finally tumbles out like an avalanche gaining speed. This is never how I saw this moment happening. "I've loved you my entire life. Do you know what that's like? To pine away for someone day after day, year after year, someone who keeps insisting that we can only be friends because she couldn't stand to lose me? Let me tell you—it's heartbreaking. And tiring. And the hardest fucking thing I've ever done, okay? And now on my wedding day, suddenly Stella says something and you open your eyes and see what's been here all along?" Her eyes don't stray from mine as the anger pours out of me. "Well, I'm sorry, it's too late. I'm getting married, Juno. I made a commitment. Not like it matters. If I canceled this wedding, you'd probably run away tomorrow. Let's just admit that this is what it is—you're jealous and scared to lose me."

She winces. "Do you have any idea what it took for me to come here right now? How scared I am that what we had has changed? I cannot live without you." Her chin drops to her chest and her tears drop to the floor.

"You don't get to make this all about you again. You're too late." I fold my arms over my chest, a million things on the tip of my tongue begging to be unleashed.

"So you're going to go through with a fake marriage?"

"I made a promise."

She nods. "Okay. Well, I guess that's it then."

"I guess so."

She walks by me, right to the door.

"Juno."

"What?"

"You'll be happy tomorrow when you realize nothing has changed with our friendship. These feelings you have for me will vanish as soon as you know you didn't lose me." I don't turn around because if I did, I'd probably cage her to the wall and confess how much I love her. How much I hope she's really had her eyes opened to how perfect we are together.

But it's all just too big of a coincidence.

She says, "I know I haven't made it easy on you all these years, and I wish I didn't harbor this fear of losing you. And yeah, I'm sure everyone, you included, think I feel this way now because I lost my parents so young and I'm scared of losing you now that you're getting married. But what's been keeping me up at night since you announced your engagement are these images in my head of you loving another woman the way you've loved me all these years. And I know I'm slow on the uptake and I should have owned my feelings for you a long time ago. I can even understand why you're angry with me, but you're wrong. Tomorrow I will still be nursing a broken heart because I do love you, Colton Stone. Every year that love has compounded, but I kept that memory of us in the treehouse on the day of my parents' funeral front and center in my mind to remind me that whatever horrible thing happens in my life, you'll be there to see me through. But now, the horrible thing that's happening to me is you marrying another woman and I haven't been able to talk to you about how badly it hurts." She pauses. "You can choose to believe me or not, but I've never lied to you."

I hear the click of the door opening and closing behind her.

My chin falls to my chest and I stuff my hands into my pockets. The jagged corners of the necklace's charm press against my fingertips. I take it out and twirl it in my hand.

Another knock on the door sounds behind me, followed by the creak of the door opening.

"It's time, Colton," Selene says.

I put the charm back into my pocket and turn to face her.

"You look very dashing," she says.

I smile, although the last thing I feel right now is happy. "Thank you."

I walk out of the room, out the door, through the garden, until I'm standing in front of the lines of white chairs. I smile at Preacher Reynolds and she smiles back.

Glancing around the small area, I see all the people who have witnessed me being raised in this town. All the Baileys, my second family, are sectioned together. Juno, pretending to be busy on her phone, sits with Jason next to her.

I try to picture myself in her position and I can't. I'm not sure I could ever see her marry someone else.

The music starts, and as everyone turns to watch Brigette walk down the aisle, Juno looks at me. Our gazes lock and her green eyes reflect everything I'm feeling.

I shouldn't have lashed out at her. To know Juno is to know how much it took for her to come to me.

Before I can blink, Brigette's standing at the altar in front of me in her simple white dress with no veil. She looks like a bride, but she doesn't beam. There's no love between us. This is a business transaction. One I hoped to use to finally force myself to move on from the dream of Juno being mine someday. How did I think I could go through with this?

Preacher Reynolds smiles at us, and Brigette passes her bouquet to my mom since we opted not to have bridesmaids or groomsmen. Brigette holds out her hands and my gaze strays to Juno once again. She's yet to actually look at the two of us, her head turned toward the ground as if she's picking a piece of lint off her dress.

Brigette continues to hold her hands out for me to take so we can say our vows. "Colton?"

Fuck, I made a mess for myself.

"I'm sorry," I say. "I can't marry you."

Brigette blinks rapidly a few times then nods. She doesn't ask any questions. She just turns and walks down the aisle back into the Cozy Cottage B&B.

I hear a gasp from the crowd. All the guests' eyes follow her before returning to fix on me.

"Colton?" my mom asks softly, concern thick in her voice.

I stand in front of our guests and swallow the lump in my throat. "I'm very sorry, everyone. There will not be a wedding today. I apologize for the inconvenience. Thank you all for coming." I bow my head and walk down the aisle, past all the whispers. I stop at the end of the aisle. "Please stay and eat. The food is paid for already."

I'm not sure what I expected to feel when I walked out of my wedding, but I sure as hell didn't expect to feel relieved.

NINETEEN

Colton

I knock on Brigette's door, and she tells me to come in. She's already taken down her hair, and she sits at the window that overlooks Selene's garden.

I walk in, rubbing my hands together, and sit on the edge of the bed. "I'm sorry."

"You said that," she says. "This is about Juno?"

"Yes... no... I don't know." It's the truth. I'm not sure what will happen with Juno, but as I stood at that altar, I knew I couldn't marry someone I don't love. I do really want to help Brigette, she's a friend, but if Juno is ready to confess her love to me, I can't throw it away no matter how angry I am that she chose now to tell me.

"It's funny. I almost didn't show up this morning," Brigette says, sounding resolved.

"Why?"

She turns in her chair to face me. "Because you love her. And I don't say that out of anger, but I'm not an evil person, Colton. I can't let you throw your entire life away just so I don't have to go back to France."

"But you did show up," I say.

She nods. "I convinced myself that we'd come to some kind of agreement. Figure it out. Maybe we could tell Juno eventually. But that's no life for you or her. I was just being selfish."

"What will you do now?"

She shrugs, taking more bobby pins out of her hair. "Go back to France, I suppose, but first I think I might go on a date."

"With who?" I figure it's either Rhys or Jason. I'm not sure which one she likes.

"Rhys has been bringing his dog in a lot. We ran into each other last night and—"

I hold up my hand. "Say no more."

Whatever she did is her own business. This was never a relationship.

"I'm not this person," she says. "I'm sorry for ever putting you in this position."

I stand and take her hands, helping her to her feet before I hug her. "I agreed to it. I guess it all sounded easier than it ended up being in reality. I thought I could do it. I was angry at Juno at the time and desperate to move on with my life. But we were in this together."

She turns around and pulls up her hair. "Do you mind?" I unzip her dress, and she turns back around. "Thank you. And thank you for everything, Colton. You're a good man."

"So you don't hate me?"

She disappears behind a changing screen, and the wedding dress comes to lay over the top of the divider. "No. I could never hate you. You stopped our wedding for love. It's noble." She peeks out, only showing her head. "But I do hope it ends happily for you."

I'm not telling her about Juno coming to me before the wedding. I'd hate for her to be mad at Juno, though it sounds to me as if Brigette's found someone she has feelings for anyway.

"Come down and have a drink."

She comes out from behind the divider wearing yoga pants and a short T-shirt that shows her stomach. "No, those are your friends."

"They can be yours too. They're good people."

She smiles. "No, you go. Maybe dance with the woman you should have been marrying in the first place." She raises her eyebrows.

"You'll be okay?" I stand by the door. It was hard not to run to Juno, pick her up over my shoulder, and leave with her as soon as I left the altar, but I had to settle things with Brigette first. Now that I have, I can't wait to see Juno.

"I'll be fine. Go."

"You'll let me know if you need anything?" I stop with the door open.

"I'm not your responsibility anymore. Go get your girl."

I nod and shut the door, thankful Brigette is being so cool about the whole thing. Still, I feel bad for not following through on my commitment.

I jog down the stairs, but when I get to the bottom, I find my mom and dad sitting in Selene's living room. They stand as I reach the final stair.

"I need to tell you both something."

Neither of my parents are stern, but I haven't done a lot in my life to upset them. Other than missing a few curfews when I was at the Baileys'. I'm not sure how they'll react to the truth.

"How is Brigette?" my mom asks, sitting back down when I sit on the chair across from them.

"She's good. She understands."

"Colt, I'm confused. You've been engaged for months. What happened?" my dad asks.

"Brigette's student visa was expiring..."

My dad's hand runs along his forehead.

My mom's forehead crinkles. "I don't understand."

"He was marrying her so she could get a green card," my dad says, and I can tell he's not happy.

"What? Really?"

I nod.

"Jesus, son, do you have any idea how much you put yourself at risk?" Dad asks. "It's not something to mess with. You could have gone to jail if anyone found out."

"Did Juno know?" my mom asks.

I shake my head, and she diverts her gaze to the fireplace.

"I know. I know. But Brigette needed the help, and I agreed to it." They don't need to know all the reasons why.

"Stupid. Just plain stupid, son. You're a smart boy, but damn, this was a stupid decision. Thank God you didn't go through with it." My dad's head doesn't stop shaking.

"Why didn't you?" my mom asks. "I mean, you took it this far."

"Is this why you wouldn't let us pay for anything?" my dad asks. "You could have told us."

My mom puts her hand on my dad's arm. "Hold on,

Rich." She squares her eyes on me. "Why did you call off the wedding? Is it what I told you in the painting room?"

I shake my head. "No, but next time I'm going to marry someone, let's try not to tell me you think I should be marrying someone else."

Mom just smiles. "As long as it's Juno, I won't be saying anything of the kind. I knew something was off. You've loved Juno your entire life, then suddenly this French woman comes to town and you're going to marry her? I might not have figured out the green card thing, but a mom senses when her son is doing something he shouldn't."

I run my hand behind my neck.

"Juno is his best friend," my dad says.

My mom stares at me and tilts her head, waiting for me to tell my dad. "Tell him."

She's really something else.

"Well, I'm not going to talk to you guys about this until I talk to her," I say.

"Are you telling me that the whole time you two were hanging out all the time you were..."

"No, Rich, they were blind to it. Well, I don't think Colton was, but Juno, you know, with Tim and Beth..."

This is how it goes in my house. We never actually talk about how the Baileys died.

My dad nods because he knows the drill. "Do you even know if she loves you?"

I stand, unable to continue having this conversation with them. I want to pull Juno aside and kiss her, tell her that I'm sorry for the way I acted, and start over. "Can we table this conversation?"

My mom must understand because she nods with way too big of a smile on her face for having a son who just called off his wedding. "Go, honey."

I walk out the sliding door to the porch and head toward the white tent. Based on the music and sounds of conversation, most guests stayed.

Standing at the edge of the tent, I watch Juno for a moment. The first thing I notice is Jason is gone and she's huddled in a corner, talking with her sisters. As if she senses me, she looks up and our eyes catch. I step forward into the tent.

Dr. Murphy steps in front of me. "Colton."

"Dr. Murphy."

"How is Brigette?" he asks.

"She's good. I think we were both in agreement."

He puts out his hand between us and I shake it. "I didn't think you were going to come to your senses. Marrying someone for a green card isn't exactly something I ever saw you doing."

"Wha—what?"

He laughs. "You think the government wouldn't contact your employer? It took me a while, but after they called and asked about the authenticity of your relationship, I watched the way you guys interacted a little closer. Only small amounts of affection, and only in front of others. I'd enter the break room and the two of you would be on opposite sides of the table. I never even heard you sneaking into the supply closet. I mean, you were newly engaged." He winks.

"Man." I shake my head.

He grips my hand harder. "Four Paws is yours. We'll draw up the paperwork next week."

"Really?"

He nods. "Yes, and I have a friend in immigration. Let me see what I can do about Brigette."

"Thanks, Dr. Murphy."

He slides his hand out of mine. "You're a good boy, Colton."

Dr. Murphy looks across the way at Juno then back at me. He smiles and pats me on the back, then walks away.

I step onto the makeshift dance floor with a huge lump in my throat. Juno looks through the space between two sisters' shoulders and her lips lift into a smile the closer I come.

Part of me wants to run to her, and another part wants to savor this moment. A moment I've waited years for. We're finally going to step over that line she drew so long ago.

"Colton!" Kingston steps in front of me, and Juno's smile disappears.

He pushes on my chest until we're out of the tent, away from everyone else—and where apparently all the rest of the Bailey brothers are waiting for us. Austin's hands are in his pockets. Rome's arms are crossed. Denver's open palm has his other fist in it.

Kingston grabs my shoulder and squeezes. "You call off your wedding and now you give our sister googly eyes? What the hell is wrong with you, man?"

"Do you really think we trust you with our sister after you almost married someone else?" Rome asks.

Denver just stands there, hammering his fist into his open palm over and over, glaring at me.

"Think about it, Colton. Give us one reason we should be okay with you and our sister?" Kingston says.

They cannot be serious. I never thought I'd have to worry about them being okay with me and Juno. Shit. I underestimated them. "I'm in love with her."

"You're in love with her?" Kingston echoes my words back at me. "Do we believe him?"

Austin rocks back on his heels. "I do." A smile breaks his serious facade.

"Fuck yeah. About time." Denver pretends to punch me in the stomach.

"I wondered what the hell you were thinking." Rome puts me in a headlock and his knuckles rub my scalp.

"But in all seriousness, if you hurt her, we'll fuck you up," Kingston says with a smile.

"I'm not going to hurt her."

"We know," Austin says and nods toward the tent. "As messed up as this situation is, go talk to her."

"Thanks."

I walk away from the four Bailey brothers and step into the tent for the second time. Now Juno is standing with Calista, Dion, and Phoebe, dancing in a circle.

"The Difference" by Tyler Rich comes over the speakers, and I hold my hand out to Juno. "Dance with me?"

Rome's three kids stare at me as if they don't recognize me.

Juno slides her hand into mine and I pull her toward me.

"Is this weird? Do you think people are staring?" she says, her gaze darting across the room.

I place my finger under her chin and raise her head until our eyes meet. "All I care about is us." I put one hand around her small waist and hold her hand between our chests. "I'm sorry for earlier."

She shakes her head, tears welling in her eyes. "I should apologize. It was your wedding, and I ruined it."

"Thankfully. Otherwise I might have been dancing with the wrong girl right now."

"Colton, what if..."

I shake my head. "Just live in this moment. Forget every-one. It's just me and you. No one else."

She lays her head against my chest. "I love you."

My chest swells and feels as buoyant as a helium-filled balloon. I kiss the top of her head. "I love you."

No other words have ever felt so good leaving my mouth. I hold her tighter—and now that I have her, I'm never letting her go.

TWENTY

Juno

Colton guides me out of the tent after we danced. Everyone snapped pictures, and you can be sure one of them will probably end up on Buzz Wheel.

"Where are we going?" I ask.

"We're going to my house."

"But what about..."

He stops us a few feet from the B&B, his large hands cradling my cheeks, his tender eyes examining mine. "Everything is taken care of. My parents will handle any loose ends. But I'm not spending the night with you at my canceled wedding reception. Where's Jason?"

"I sent him home. Told him I couldn't see him anymore." I step closer so that our chests meet. "Kiss me, Colton."

Other than saying he loved me and holding me like a

cherished gift on the dance floor, we haven't stepped over that line.

"Words I've wanted to hear for too long." He smiles and bends down, placing his lips on mine.

I wind my arms around his neck, our bodies pressed together. The night has grown colder, and all the insects that call Selene's garden home chirp and buzz around us. The music flowing from the tent—where we left Grandma Dori doing the cha-cha—can't cover all the noise as nature comes alive at night.

His tongue slips against mine and his hands fall from my face, wrapping around my waist. I've kissed Colton many times before. At thirteen, when neither one of us knew what we were doing. At eighteen, when we'd each had some practice. At twenty-six, when I realized he'd grown up and knew how to kiss a woman. But none of those kisses felt as right as this one. And just like that, his lips on mine make my knees almost give out.

He breaks it off too soon and his hand slides into mine, tugging me across the yard. "We need to get home."

"Colton." I stop him as he fiddles in his pocket for his keys. "How is Brigette? Is she upset?"

When Colton said he couldn't marry her, I felt guilty that my first reaction was joy. Because with my joy came her hurt, and if I'd owned my feelings earlier, she would have never been caught in the middle.

"She's good. She understood, and I think she might have been a little relieved. Dr. Murphy said he's going to talk to a friend of his at the immigration office." He unlocks his truck and puts his hand on my hip. "But that's the last time I want to hear her name tonight, okay?" He tucks a loose hair behind my ear. "I've waited too long to have you here with me like this."

I rise up on my tiptoes. "Okay, but if you ever omit information from me again, we're going to have a throw-down. Got it?" I push my finger into his chest.

After I laid all my hidden feelings at Colton's feet, a despair I haven't felt in a long time filled my chest. Add on the fact that he was marrying her for a green card, and it made my pain worse. But then, how can I be that upset? His fake marriage forced me to get my head out of my ass.

"I'll never keep another secret from you." He kisses me. "Now please get in the truck."

I giggle and climb in. He rounds the front, shrugging off his jacket and loosening his tie. As he climbs in, he tosses his jacket into the back seat, starting the truck. Our situation is no different than all the other times I've been in his truck before, but at the same time, it is. His intention this time is to take me to his house so we can have sex.

He pulls out onto the road and I watch the scenery go by.

"This is weird, right?" I look at him and he turns his head, but I can't read him. "I mean, you were going to marry someone else and now we're going back to your house to do it."

He pulls to the side of the road and puts it in park. "Do you not want to go to my house? Would you rather take this slower?" My nerves set in as he takes my hands. "You can run this. Hell, I've waited this long. A few more weeks isn't going to make my balls any bluer than they already are. But if you have some stipulation about so many dates we need to have before we sleep together, then you better free up your calendar for the foreseeable future."

He's got it all wrong. I want to have sex with him. He's played the starring role in my dreams for months now. "I don't want to take it slower. I was just thinking that the last time we had sex, we had both had our fair share of alcohol..." I shrug. "It just seems weird that I'm going to see your penis."

"You've seen it before. And can we not call it a penis? It sounds like we're in that puberty class in the fifth grade."

I chuckle. "I know, I know. But don't you feel weird that you're going to see me naked?"

"Um, no. I feel eager. I have puzzle pieces of you that I've formed in my head and I can't wait to see the whole package stone-cold sober."

I unbuckle my seat belt and rise onto my knees, leaning forward to kiss him again. "You always say all the right things." I press my lips to his. "Take me home. Forget what I said."

Getting situated in the seat again, I clasp my seat belt and he puts the truck in drive.

"What if I'm not what you imagined?" I say as he pulls into his neighborhood.

Colton lives just outside downtown so he can walk to work if he wants. It's a two-story, three-bedroom house that people made fun of him for buying when he graduated vet school. He told me he didn't want to move into an apartment and pay someone else's mortgage. We looked at thirty houses before he put an offer on this one. Watching Brigette move in and make it her home after I helped him decorate it all these years probably would have felt like a knife in my heart.

He says nothing until he's parked in his garage and takes the keys out of the ignition.

"I'm gonna need you to get out of your head now." He climbs out of the truck, and I open my door to climb out, but he's there to open it for me. "From now on, you wait until I open it for you."

"That's demanding, and you know I don't adhere to demands," I say, accepting his hand to step down onto the running board then the concrete.

He chuckles. "Okay. Please don't get out of the truck before I can open the door from this point forward? Is that better?"

I walk into his house. "Maybe, but I can open my own door. Just saying."

I do love his chivalry. He's always been that way throughout our friendship. But I also like giving him a hard time.

I slide off my heels in his laundry room and walk into his kitchen like any other time I've come here. I'm smiling until I spot the folder on the table labeled honeymoon. "Oh, you were going on a honeymoon?"

He picks up the folder and stuffs it into a drawer. "Just a quick trip in case questions were asked. With no cancellation insurance so I guess I can kiss that money goodbye."

"Do you think you guys would have... I mean, maybe feelings would have developed."

"No. I don't." He rounds the kitchen table and grabs my hand, entwining our fingers. "I was already in love with a crazy ginger."

"But over time?"

"Stop it." He releases my hands and wraps his around my waist, pulling me to him.

"Stop what?"

He kisses my forehead. "Stop trying to put roadblocks in the way of what's happening between us."

"I'm not."

"I see it. It's the same way you were after we had sex right before I left for college."

My forehead falls to his chest. This man sees through me and it scares me. "I think I'm just scared."

His lips press to the top of my head. "Me too, but I don't want to be anywhere else. Do you?"

I look up at him, willing myself to push past the fear. "No."

His knuckles graze my cheek. "Look, we're already agreeing."

He bends down and kisses me. The awkwardness fades, and an intense desire for this man replaces any hesitation. I want more as he sweeps his tongue into my mouth and his fingers thread through my hair, holding my head to him. As if I'd pull away now.

My hands fiddle with his shirt, unbuttoning each button until his chest is bare. If I could stand to have his lips off me, I'd push him back so I could watch my hands slide down his well-built chest.

He strips his lips off mine, eyes searching my dress. "Zipper?"

"Side." I push his shirt off his shoulders.

He takes a moment to remove his cufflinks, then he's standing in front of me shirtless. It's not anything I haven't seen before—the man runs down Main Street without a shirt on during the hottest days of summer—but I can't look away.

"I love the way you're looking at me." He steps forward, his fingers finding the zipper of my dress and we stare at one another as he lowers the zipper down my body. "You're gorgeous."

"Colton," I say, shutting my eyes as his hands move the straps off and down my arms.

"Just tell me if you want me to stop."

I shake my head. My dress pools at my waist, needing

one final push before it puddles to the floor around my ankles. I open my eyes and Colton's gaze is locked on my chest, his tongue sliding along his bottom lip, taking in my bare breasts.

I couldn't find a bra that wouldn't show under the dress, so I stand in front of him wearing only sheer black panties. Picking me up by the hips, he props me up on the table.

"I've wanted you for so long." His knuckles graze down my chest, over my peaked nipples.

He bends, his mouth casting small open-mouth kisses down the center of my breasts. His tongue slides over my right nipple before he sucks it. I grip the back of his head to hold him there, and he twirls the pebbled nub with his tongue then blows his hot breath over it.

"Should we take this upstairs?" he whispers, his mouth moving back up to mine.

"Yes." He sweeps me up with one arm, and I lock my legs around his waist. "You're going to find this crazy, but a small part of me expected us to be fumbling and for you to not be so suave and manly."

He rears his head back, midway up the stairs. "Are you saying you didn't think I had skills?"

I put my finger on his lips. "I don't want to hear the stories of how you got all these seduction skills."

He chuckles and presses his lips lightly to my mine. "Okay, I won't tell you."

"Wait... do I want to know?"

He walks us into his bedroom with the navy blue walls that I helped paint. After lowering me onto the taupe comforter we argued about at the store for ten minutes, he ventures to the side table of the matching furniture that we each agreed on the minute we saw it at the store.

He pulls out a condom and tosses it on top of the

dresser before his fingers move to his belt. Here we go. I'm going to see his penis. I mean cock.

"Open your eyes, Juno," he says.

I giggle and peek through one eye. His zipper coming down is as loud as if it were a fire alarm. His belt buckle landing on the hardwood floor has my other eye opening. He wears a pair of black boxer briefs and his dick is bulging out of them.

But as he puts his fingers to the waistband to pull them down, I hold up my hand to stop him. "Wait!"

The longer I look at him, the more my nerves turn into something electrifying. I get up on my knees, his tongue licking his bottom lip as he watches me cat-crawl toward him.

"I take it you're not freaked out anymore?" he asks as I sit back on my heels in front of him.

"Quite the opposite." I palm his length over his boxers.

His hand slides to the back of my head, then he dips down and captures my lips in a kiss that's definitely more than friends.

And finally, my head flips from thinking of Colton as just my best friend from childhood to accepting the sexy, mouth-watering guy he is.

TWENTY-ONE

Colton

Juno palming my dick is something I can definitely get used to. The vision of her cat-crawling to me wearing only a pair of black panties now has a permanent spot on the highlight reel. Her hand slides into my boxers and she grabs my dick. I groan, thrusting into her hand.

She dips her tongue into my mouth and my other hand holds her head, so she doesn't stop what she's doing. Her grip on me tightens, and she pumps her fist up and down my dick.

God, the noises she makes. One thing I took from our night two years ago was how loud she gets. But there's no Kingston in the bedroom next door tonight, and each moan that slips from her lips is a sign that she's in this moment with me.

I push one hand into her panties, stroking her slowly. Damn, she's wet.

Eventually frantic need takes over and she manages to get my boxer briefs down my thighs. She strips her lips off mine, her fingers flowing down my chest from ridge to ridge.

"I want you," she says, sliding to the side to grab the condom.

She must be crazy. I took the condom out for easy access, not because I want to rush tonight. I take her out from behind her knees and her back falls to the mattress before she can reach the condom.

"Hey!"

Raising one of her legs in the air, I kiss my way up from her ankle before lightly biting her inner thigh. "It's not time yet."

I stare at her between her legs and watch her chest rise and fall. I hook her leg over my shoulder and lick her pussy through her soaked sheer panties. Taking my index finger, I slide her panties aside, exposing her to me. She arches her back off the mattress, squirming and pressing her center closer to my mouth. I nudge her thighs open wider, teasing her with my finger, never fully inserting it as my tongue twirls her nub and I suck it into my mouth. She's wiggling along the mattress, her tits bouncing, her breaths becoming shallower with every inhale.

I want to set a world record for how many times she comes tonight, whether it's from my dick, tongue, or fingers.

Slowly, I push my finger into her and withdraw it, following the signs her body gives me, trying to read what she enjoys and never pushing the tempo too fast.

Her hands fall to my comforter and fist it. I watch her from between her legs, plunging another finger inside her, arching them to massage her G-spot. Our eyes lock when she inches up off the bed to watch me, then her eyes fall closed and flutter back open, her tits rising and falling with every breath.

"Oh my God," she says, collapsing on the mattress.

She bucks against my mouth and her entire body tenses, her pussy clenching around my fingers before her hands finally release my comforter. A deep, satisfied sigh slips from her lips.

I need to get inside her right now. After grabbing the condom off the nightstand, I sit up on my knees, tearing the package open and sliding the rubber down my length. Juno's on the pill, but I'm not going to assume she's ready to go bare on our first night together.

I cast kisses up her stomach, over her rose tattoo, through the valley of her breasts, until I reach her mouth. "Recovered yet?"

Her eyes flicker to awareness and the smallest smile creases her lips. "Man, you have skills I should've been taking advantage of a long time ago."

"Don't worry, you have plenty of time now." I kiss the corner of her lips. I don't want us to relive regrets of time wasted because all I care about now is our future.

The tip of my cock hits her center and she moans, widening her legs. Her arms wrap around my body and she gasps when our bare chests press together. I push inside her, and her fingers fiddle with my hair, playing leisurely. I think she's enjoying the slow pace I'm setting.

"I hope you're ready to be sore tomorrow," I say before my tongue slips into her mouth.

I'm not interested in her answer. Her legs wrapping around my waist is answer enough that she's on board.

I've been in this exact position with Juno before—when we were drunk. That night it was more about the destination than the journey, but tonight is *all* about the journey.

My hands push her hair out of her face while my lips sprinkle kisses on any skin I can reach while still being buried deep inside her. My pace increases as her heels press into my calves and incoherent words tumble out of her mouth.

"I'll never get enough of you," I say.

Her hands move to my shoulder blades, her fingers digging into my muscles. "Don't stop."

She arches her neck and my mouth devours the skin like a starved man, sucking and nipping. Her hips rise to meet mine and I thrust into her, my hands unable to stop touching her silky skin.

I can't believe how fast she went from Juno my friend, to Juno my lover. I love her. I always have, but in this bed, I know that everything we were before tonight will never compare to what we'll be. A fire sparks in me, and I bury my head in Juno's neck, thrusting over and over, chasing my own pleasure.

"I'm coming," she pants in my ear. Her fingernails dig hard into my shoulder blades.

I don't increase my pace, waiting for her to clench around me before I chase my own orgasm. As if on cue, her thighs tighten around my waist and she cries out in my ear, singing my praises. I thrust harder into her until a million asteroids break apart into little stars behind my eyelids and I empty myself inside her.

The weight of my body falls on top of her and I have never felt this at peace.

Rising up on my elbows, I stare at her. Her skin is flushed and she's still catching her breath. "Still weird?"

She hits my back. "Turns out I quite like your penis."

I kiss her lips. "Can we please stop calling it my penis now?"

"Do you want me to come up with a name for it?"

I pull out of her, and sure enough, I'm still at half-mast, almost ready to go again. "I was thinking more just cock or dick."

I sit up and she stretches her arms over her head. Her naked body is still bare for me to worship. "I feel like you want me to name it Anaconda or something."

"We could just go with Boss." I laugh, heading into the bathroom to dispose of the condom.

When I come back, Juno's digging through my drawer for a T-shirt. She pulls one out and moves to my shorts drawer. We're so comfortable together, how will we keep this dating stage new and exciting?

I sit on the edge of the bed, admiring her ass as she's bent over. She turns around and I put my arms out for her to come to me. She does. Hopefully, this is a good sign that she's over being uncomfortable with the idea of us being naked together.

"Do you want a shirt?" She holds out the one she already has in her hands.

"No. You can wear my shirt, but I'll take the shorts."

"Let me grab you a pair."

I shake my head. "You're going to wear my T-shirt without anything underneath."

She smiles and wraps her arms around my neck. "Why?"

"Because all the times I sat there and watched you in my shorts and shirt, I always wished you were only wearing my shirt and nothing else."

"So this is like a fantasy?" She grins.

"Do you have any fantasies?"

She shrugs, climbing off my lap and putting on the T-shirt.

"Whoa, whoa, whoa." I grab the hem and pull her toward me, my hands sliding up her chest. "I didn't say to put the shirt on now."

"I'm starving and I'm not going to eat naked."

I let the T-shirt fall and snatch the shorts off the bed, stepping into them. "How about some *9 ½ Weeks* action?"

"You know I've never seen that movie?" She glances back at me before disappearing out of my bedroom.

"That's changing right now." We walk down the stairs and I slide my arms around her waist, pulling her back to me, making it difficult for us to get to the kitchen. "I think I beat off to that movie every day the summer after I turned fourteen."

She circles around, and I pick her up, her legs winding around my waist. "Hmm... and here I thought maybe you only beat off to me?"

"Well, you were still flat-chested then." She hits my back and I put her on the kitchen counter, my hands sliding up her thighs to part them, my fingers dangerously close to her center. "Don't worry, you're number one."

She rolls her eyes. "I'm flattered."

I open the fridge. Unfortunately, I haven't really gone grocery shopping this week because I anticipated being away for my honeymoon.

"I don't have much." I set eggs on the counter behind me and a pizza I ordered last night but never finished.

"Tell me something you imagine about me when you're jerking off."

I glance over my shoulder and cock an eyebrow. "Is that your kink?"

She shrugs. "There were times that I... you know..."

I abandon the fridge and nestle my hips between her legs again. "No, I don't know. I'll tell you if you tell me."

A blush runs up her neck, hitting her cheeks.

"You don't have to be shy with me." I pull her to the edge of the counter and her arms fall over my shoulders.

"You tell me first."

I nod. "Well, I fantasized about you wearing my T-shirts with nothing on underneath, like I said, but there was this one night when I returned from college before I started graduate school. I was at your apartment and the air went out. Kingston had been called to a fire, so he was gone. You guys were letting me crash until I found a place of my own. It started to rain, and you thought the cool rain would feel good because we were both so hot even with all the fans on us. Do you remember?"

She nods and smiles. "We went outside, and I realized way too late I was wearing white. You said you didn't notice." She slaps my chest and I laugh.

"Because if I had told you, you would've wanted to go inside. But..." I lean forward and press a kiss to her lips. "I always have this fantasy that I approach you, take off your T-shirt and shorts, and we have sex right there as the rain pours down over us."

"In the middle of downtown?" Her eyebrows rise.

"That's why it's a fantasy. It was just us, the rain, and a desolate street."

She wiggles. "I like that one." I wait patiently until she stares at me. "What?"

"Your turn."

She gnaws at the inside of her cheek. "Mine is actually from this house."

"Do tell." I open the pizza box and take out a slice, holding it to her lips.

She takes a small bite, chews, and swallows. "I came over one day, and I think it was summer too. You were working on the deck. And you had shorts on, no shirt, and a tool belt. Your chest was so shiny with sweat and your muscles would flex and bulge with every swing of the hammer."

"What's the fantasy? Because from what I remember, you threw me a water, I scrambled to catch it, and you said it was too hot to be outside."

She giggles and nods. "Well, that night, let's just say, that tool belt dropped to the wooden deck, along with your shorts, and you showed me your real tool."

"I'm not sure which one is better." I feed her more of the slice of pizza.

"Mine of course." She nudges close to me, kissing up my jawline. "Your five o'clock shadow is looking pretty hot right now."

"Why, Miss Nympho, are you wanting to take this pizza upstairs?"

She shakes her head. "I never said upstairs. Besides, I think I have to get to know your penis a little better so I can properly nickname it." Her fingers sweep down my chest until they slip under the elastic of my shorts.

"Can we please just use dick in the meantime?" Her palm applies pressure and I rock against it. "On second thought, call it whatever you want as long as you keep doing that."

And in only a few hours, we christen two rooms in my house. Thank goodness I bought a three-bedroom.

TWENTY-TWO

Juno

A large arm slips around my waist, fingers crawling up my stomach, cradling me into a strong chest.

"Morning," Colton says in a groggy voice.

I'm not sure if we're actually up or only temporarily awake for our sixth time tonight. Neither one of us has allowed the other to sleep. After the kitchen, we tried to watch a movie, but that just ended with me on my knees between his legs. Then a movie in bed sounded like a better plan, but five minutes in, Colton was kissing my neck and his hands were venturing south to my core. And every time we rolled around in the bed, one of us found the other and a few groggy kisses turned into sex.

He rolls over me, his length already hard and ready. Locking my wrists down with his strong hands, he teases his tip at my center. We're already done with condoms and if I'm being honest, I wasn't sure we'd even use them to begin with. Last night in the kitchen when the condom seemed a million miles away, we had a brief talk about testing and he already knew I was on the pill.

Weird because in a way, I feel as if we've warped past a million stages of a normal relationship.

"Mr. Willy is already up and raring to go with the sun, huh?"

He shakes his head, but his smirk says he doesn't hate the new names I'm trying out for his dick. For some reason, it's easier than acknowledging that we've crossed that line and I'm now way too familiar with the way my best friend screws.

I widen my legs to give his hips more room and he slides into my wetness. I moan softly as if I'm a cat being pampered. Without releasing my hands, he grinds into me, circling his hips in a painfully slow motion. One thing that's consistent is Colton's always looking at me to see what I'm enjoying. I've noticed he can read my body, which has to be a perk of him knowing me so well.

"Will I ever not want to be woken up like this?" I arch my back, tugging at my hands, wanting to touch him.

"I hope not." He bends down and kisses me, his tongue more confident than the first time we kissed last night. As though he's already used to kissing me in less than twenty-four hours. Just when I think he's going to release my hands, he closes the kiss, placing one last one on the tip of my nose.

"I need my hands," I say.

He laughs and shakes his head. "You don't."

He thrusts harder and my back arches off the bed. He takes the opportunity to close his mouth over my nipple and suck on my breast. I can't argue with that.

His mouth pops off and he increases his tempo in and out of me. I wiggle my wrists, but he doesn't remove his restraint and there's something about not being able to touch him, about being held down, that I'm enjoying way too much. His lips fall over my bare skin, teasing, nibbling, and sucking as he grinds in and out of me. I wrap my legs around his waist, the only control I have, and tighten my thighs around his middle. It makes the friction that much better.

A ripple of an orgasm stirs in my belly, and I chase the high swirling around me. "Harder," I say, panting, content to struggle with my wrists locked on the bed.

For a moment, I'm lost in his love-filled eyes. As scared as I am about this going south, there's no one else I'd rather be with. His eyes catch mine, and whatever he sees causes him to release my wrists. His hands land on my face and he kisses me as though it's our first time, never breaking pace.

Somewhere between his tongue sliding into the depths of my mouth and my hands being able to explore his body, he carries me to the edge of the cliff. In the last twelve hours, I've seen stars, he's made me come so hard and so fast. I've been dizzy with lust, needy to have another one. But this time, a sense of peace falls over my body. And as he stills inside me, I hold his body to mine, taking the weight of the love and safety only he can give me.

Propping up on his elbows, he stares at me. "Now that is a good morning."

He kisses my lips, withdraws out of me, and heads to the bathroom. The messy side of not using a condom kind of sucks, but the gentleman he is, he returns with a washcloth for me.

I clean up then get up from the bed and head into the bathroom. "If we don't want to have our own little one, I'd better get home to take my pill."

He follows and turns on the water to the shower. "How

about I make some dresser space for you here?"

I stare at him through my reflection in the mirror. "Isn't that moving fast?"

"I see it more like moving slow."

He comes up behind me and kisses my neck. That sense of belonging fills my chest again and radiates outward. I'm not sure about taking over dresser space though.

I circle around in his arms. "Let's talk about it after at least a week." I giggle and kiss his cheek. "I'm starving. While you shower, I'm going to make us something."

He walks into his glass-doored shower. "Did you forget you don't cook? Plus, I need groceries. Want to go grocery shopping?"

"I'm not really sure I want to be in public after last night? I'm the *other* woman." I put some toothpaste on my finger and run it over my teeth and tongue, then spit in the sink and cup my hand for some water.

"I think Brigette was always the other woman according to Lake Starlight residents."

"Speaking of, did you check online?"

"Buzz Wheel?" he asks as I watch soap travel down the contours of his body. There're no traces of the boy I grew up with—he's all man now. "No. I don't care what it has to say."

"I wonder if it went up last night or if it will be up today." I chew on my nails.

This isn't something I want in the gossip blog. Of course the Bailey who breaks up a wedding is me. Why should this situation be any different than the rest of my life? It's always been *one of these things is not like the other*.

"It doesn't matter what it says. It changes nothing and besides, someone else will be the story tomorrow."

"How can you be so casual about this? Aren't you worried? I match people for a living and now I stole the groom of a client I matched. It's hardly an endorsement." I sit up on the counter, my stomach not rumbling with hunger anymore.

The water turns off and Colton grabs a towel from a hook on the wall. One hook, one towel. For some reason, that makes my mind shift into a completely different direction. Which isn't really an anomaly for me.

"Was Brigette going to move in here?"

He dries himself, running the towel over his hair, then wraps it around his waist. "Okay, take a breath." He cages me to the counter like moments ago, before he smelled like fresh rainfall. "You're overthinking this. Everyone always assumed we'd be together. They're going to be happy. And Brigette understands."

"Because she was marrying you for a green card, but the rest of Lake Starlight doesn't know that. They'll probably look at me like I'm a whore."

He chuckles. "They will not. Lake Starlight loves their matchmaker and they aren't going to nail you to the cross or make you wear a scarlet letter." He disappears into his room and returns with his phone. He looks at me as I put the T-shirt he gave me last night over my head. "Want me to read it or you want to read it yourself?"

I snatch the phone from him and sit on the bed, inhaling then exhaling a large breath.

LAKE STARLIGHT BUZZ Wheel

FOR THOSE NOT IN attendance at the wedding of Colton Stone last night, you might be surprised to be waking up to the news that the wedding never happened. Guests, including the entire Bailey clan, watched the bride walk down the aisle, but before vows were exchanged, the bride was walking back up the aisle, disappearing into the Cozy Cottage B&B. Colton followed but told the guests to stick around for the meal. A half hour later, Colton entered the tent only to have his first dance with—Juno Bailey. Rumors are they left the wedding together shortly after. Yes, ladies and gentlemen of Lake Starlight, the matchmaker finally succumbed to her love for Colton Stone. It's nice to see love won out last night in Lake Starlight.

SOME OF YOU might be wondering about Brigette... she was seen leaving the Cozy Cottage B&B with Rhys from Smokin' Guns Tattoo Parlor, who escorted her to his vehicle. This had a lot of guests at the wedding wondering what exactly was the cause of the canceled wedding?

I CLOSE out his phone and he knocks his shoulder to mine. "Not so bad, huh?"

I shake my head. There's no reason I should have worried they were going to crucify me. Maybe it's my own guilt. "It shouldn't ease my mind that she left with Rhys, but it does."

"You need to learn that it's okay for you to be happy."

I kiss his cheek. "I just feel like me getting what I want has left someone else to be banished from the country."

He chuckles. "Oh, Juno, she's fine. Obviously, she wanted to be with Rhys."

"I thought maybe her and Jason, but Rhys surprises me."

He takes off his towel as though it's the most natural

thing in the world and puts on a pair of track shorts and a T-shirt before tossing me a pair of shorts that I'll have to roll the waistband down to keep up. "Jason isn't Brigette's type. She wants someone who wants to travel and see the world. She wants to stay in America, but she wants the freedom to travel too. A doctor would never be able to give her that, but I think a guy like Rhys, someone who picked up and moved here not knowing a soul, might be the one for her. Jason is more like me—likely to buy a house large enough to fit a family before he's even found a wife." He takes my hand and leads me out of the room. "Now come on, let's grab some breakfast and go get you some clothes."

He leads me down the stairs. When we reach the bottom, I jump on his back so he can carry me into the kitchen, but he freezes in the archway and his arms loosen from my legs, making me slide down his back.

"Dori? Ethel?" he asks.

I peek around his body.

"Good morning, lovebirds." Dori's putting donuts on a plate while Ethel is pouring glasses of juice.

"How did you get in my house?" Colton asks.

Dori rounds the counter, licking powdered sugar off her fingers. "I have the keys to all my kids' houses."

"But I'm not your kid." Colton's face is stark white, and I laugh, passing him for a donut.

"You've always been my kid. Although I am a little upset that I was squeezed out of getting the two of you together. Which brings me to the point of my visit this morning."

I bite into a chocolate-frosted sprinkle donut and smile at Colton, who I think just realized what it means to be in a relationship with a Bailey. Grandma Dori doesn't know the meaning of the word space.

TWENTY-THREE

Colton

How the hell did Dori get a key to my house?

The question runs over and over in my head as Juno sits at the table, working on her second donut. I prepare coffee because Dori and Ethel only drink decaf, which they brought for themselves.

"Juno, you cannot be a slob." Dori picks up Juno's dress that I took off her body last night and lays it nicely over the back of my couch.

"I didn't leave it there, Colton did," she says, which shocks me since upstairs, she was so concerned that the town she grew up in would see her as evil for breaking up my wedding.

Dori swats her granddaughter's arm. "Stop it, Juno. I don't want to hear those things."

"Then why are you here this early in the morning? And please tell me you haven't been here long?" Juno glances at me because about a half an hour ago, she was screaming my name.

"Yes, we did just get here, which I guess we're thankful for."

Ethel's expression says maybe she would've liked to overhear us having sex. I shiver at the thought of that.

"And I'm here because I have to skip over you two now," Dori adds. "You're together, so I need to move on to Kingston. Word is that Stella Harrison was at your blind speed dating event."

Juno's head whips in my direction, but I shake my head. How on Earth would she get word of Stella? Did Dori spot her at the wedding? Everyone in Lake Starlight knows that Stella returning is the last thing Kingston needs. When it comes to her, he just doesn't think.

"I don't know what you're talking about," Juno says, and I see her fingers cross under the table.

"Juno Bailey!" Dori says.

Ethel turns around and smiles at me, sneaking another donut from the tray. Her eyes dip to my crotch and I smile politely. How long *were* they here?

"Dori, I'd like the key back," I say, interrupting her conversation.

Dori holds up her hand at me. "Just relax. I only come in when I have to. It's me, not some stalker."

I shake my head, thankful my coffee beeps that it's done. I pour myself a cup, holding up one to ask Juno if she wants one. She smiles and nods, so I pour her a cup.

"I don't really think we should involve ourselves in Kingston and Stella's business," Juno says, apparently admitting defeat.

"You're a matchmaker. You know as well as I do that they belong together," Dori says.

"Do they really?" Juno asks. "There's a lot of hurt there."

"There's a lot of hurt here." Dori signals between Juno and me. "But you two were able to work it out and screw like rabbits."

I stare blankly at Juno because what the hell am I supposed to say to that?

"Tell me you don't have a nanny cam in my house, Dori." I look into my family room, finding a vase I don't remember ever buying.

"Stop being silly," Dori says, again waving me off like a toddler who won't stop asking annoying questions.

But my parents don't even have a key to my house. The only person who does is...

"Juno, do you still have my key?" I ask.

"Colton Stone." Dori turns to me. "Forget the key thing. I don't have cameras on you. You're not that interesting of a person."

My mouth opens.

Juno laughs.

Ethel pats my arm, giving me a look that says she finds me interesting.

"Do you have her number?" Dori asks Juno.

Juno's gaze scatters along the countertops—trying to locate her phone, I think. "No." But she purses her lips. Her telltale sign that she's lying.

"You're lying," Dori says.

"No, I'm not," Juno says and again purses her lips. She might as well give up the fight.

"Well, ladies, I have to get Juno home to shower and change. Thanks for the donuts and juice," I say, trying to save her.

Juno's smile says she'll be thanking me later. I love these new perks.

"You're welcome," Ethel says, her eyes skimming down my body again.

I tuck my chair farther under the table.

"Juno, I just want to talk to her," Dori says.

"Grandma, she's not ready, okay? The last thing we need is Kingston to find out she's back before Stella can face him. You know how weak he is when it comes to her." Juno's tone and words change Dori's behavior.

Dori stares at her cup of coffee for a moment then nods. "Okay, you're right. I think I'm just a little upset that I didn't get a hand in getting you two together. I mean, I've been waiting months for this moment." Dori glances between Juno and me.

"Sorry, Grandma, but you did. I mean..." Juno tries to see where maybe she had something to do with getting us together, but the truth is she didn't.

"No, I didn't, but that's okay. I'm sure you'll need me down the road." She stands and sips her coffee, grabbing her purse. "Ethel, stop making googly eyes at Colton and let's go."

"What do you mean down the road?" Juno asks, getting up and hugging her grandma and Ethel.

"You guys have a lot more to go through. Did you really think you just admit your feelings, and everything is hunky-dory?" She laughs. "God, I love that saying."

Juno's eyebrows crinkle and she searches me out. I shake my head. This is Dori. She likes to be the matchmaker for her grandchildren, to feel as though they wouldn't have found their way without her.

"Kids are so naive," she tells Ethel, who nods. "They think everything is easy-peasy."

Both women walk down the hall, and I put my arm around Juno.

"The key, Dori?" I try one more time.

"See you kids later." She opens the door for Ethel, and they leave, shutting the door behind them.

"You're getting that key back," I say to Juno.

She laughs. "You're so paranoid."

"Because she has a key to my house and her friend looks at me like I'm a piece of meat."

"Ethel's a vegetarian," Juno says, still laughing.

I tickle her ribs until she's squirming and begging for mercy. I swallow her laughter with a kiss.

Dori's wrong—Juno and I have this in the bag. Nothing is gonna go wrong now that we're finally a couple.

FOR THE PAST WEEK, Juno and I have been inseparable. Dr. Murphy has called me in for a meeting today and I'm hopeful it has something to do with buying the practice.

I knock on the door to his office and he looks up from the computer, waving me in.

"Colton," he says, directing me to the chair in front of his desk.

"Good morning."

"So we lost Brigette," he says and a pit forms in my stomach. "But sounds like she's happy. You both are."

"Was your friend able to help?" I ask.

"He might have, but she and Rhys left two days ago to explore the lower forty-eight. I'm not sure what their plans are."

Dr. Murphy knows more than me. Although it was an amicable split between Brigette and me, she didn't come to me to talk about it before she and Rhys set off into the sunset. I hope she's happy though.

"That leaves an opening here at the office. I have a call in to my professor friend in Anchorage with the hopes that we can get someone to help us out. But I think we should get the paperwork together. I figure you'll need to secure a loan, so why don't you finalize that, and I'll contact my lawyer?"

"Really? You're ready?" There's a strong possibility that Dr. Murphy will stay on until we find a new person and train them.

Dr. Murphy smiles and nods. "After your stint of stopping your wedding for the one you love, Mrs. Murphy has some newfound love for spontaneity, and she wants to travel. I promised her five years ago I'd slow down once I found someone I trusted, and she's been bothering me since you graduated. So here we are. That is, if you still want the practice?"

"Yes." I nod enthusiastically. No question about it, especially now that I'm with Juno. Me owning a vet practice is the security we'll need to start our life together. "Definitely."

He smiles and shakes my hand.

"Thank you, Dr. Murphy. I promise to run it with the same professionalism and caring nature you have all these years."

"Well, we do have one problem to talk about still."

I sit back in my chair, already aware of what he wants to talk about—Lori.

"Lori's my sister, and although she could get a job somewhere else with her skills, I can't just throw her out. I sense that once you're her boss, she'll ease up on you."

I rest my elbows on the arms of the chair. "I think she might hate me."

"No. She just doesn't understand new ways of doing things and I've probably allowed her too much leeway over the years. But I have to put in the paperwork that she stays on staff until she chooses or does something against the office policies."

If this is the cost of having the business, I won't argue. Lori isn't exactly youthful, so I can handle her until her retirement. "I understand, and I'm in agreement."

His expression says he appreciates that I'm being a team player. "Okay, well, call that contact at the bank, and let's get the ball rolling. Congratulations, Colton." He stands and puts his hand out again.

I stand and shake his hand. "Thank you for this opportunity."

"You're a good kid. I'm happy to see things are turning around for you." He winks.

All I can think of is Juno, and he's right. Things couldn't be better with us, and now I'm getting the practice. Life has never been better.

After I leave Dr. Murphy's office, I go to the break room and dial up Mario at the bank, hoping the paperwork won't take that long. We've already discussed everything; the question has always been when.

"Mario Arroyo," he answers.

"Hey, Mario, it's Colton Stone."

"Dr. Murphy is finally ready to retire, huh?"

I laugh. "Yeah."

"Okay, I'll draw up the loan application. Come by on your lunch if you want, or we're open until five. You can sign everything, and I'll start getting the loan processed."

Butterflies fill my stomach. I'm actually doing this. A

loan isn't ideal, but I don't have enough in savings since I purchased a house. "I'll be there at lunch."

"Perfect."

I hang up and relish that my life is finally coming together how I always wanted.

TWENTY-FOUR

Juno

I'm packing up stuff at my office to head back to the bar in Anchorage for another blind speed dating night. I've sent a text to Stella to let her know that Kingston will be there tonight, but she hasn't answered. If they both show up, I'm diving under a table.

"Ready?" Colton walks into my office looking delicious in jeans and a T-shirt that stretches over his shoulders.

"You already changed after work? All the women there are going to be wishing you were one of the dates." I add flyers and business cards for SparkFinder into the box.

"Well, then I'll have to tell them someone stole my heart already."

I shake my head, smiling at him.

"I have some good news." He sits in my office chair, twirling around like a child.

At least he has good news. My news is that maybe, just maybe, I can catch up on my rent if these blind date functions keep going so well.

"Yeah?"

"Dr. Murphy has agreed to sell me the practice."

I abandon the box and turn around to face him. "And you waited this long to tell me? When did he let you know?"

"This morning. I had to call in my loan to be processed. Signed the papers at lunch, so I'll find out in a week or so." His boyish smile shows how happy he is.

This is what he's wanted since he graduated. He knew there was no room for two vet practices in Lake Starlight, so either he buys Four Paws from Dr. Murphy when he retires, or he would have to go somewhere else to practice. This keeps him here in Lake Starlight permanently.

Other than Colton, my life is in flux, but he doesn't need to worry about my problems when all his dreams are coming true.

"I have my girl and a practice. Life is good." He leans back and puts his hands behind his head while stretching his legs out on the desk.

"And it looks good on you." I grin.

"Good enough that you maybe want to have a quickie before we leave?" His eyebrows waggle.

I laugh, breaking the distance between us and pushing his feet off the desk. "I could just hide here under the desk. No one would know what was happening if they looked through the glass."

I glance at the clock. We have at least ten minutes before we have to leave to be there. After I slide under the desk, Colton straightens the chair so he's facing my desk straight-on. On my knees, I unbutton his jeans and pull the zipper down.

He groans and slides down in the chair so I have more to work with. Rubbing his hard length, I lower his boxer briefs down over his dick, not thinking anything of seeing it anymore. This past week, we've sought and found every erogenous zone on one another. I run my tongue up his length, twirling it around the tip, which makes him press his back to the chair.

"Shit," he says, his hands gripping the arms of my office chair.

I'm not exactly a pro at this, but Colton makes me feel like a porn star when I go down on him. He groans as one of my hand plays with his balls while my other one pumps him. My mouth works his tip as though it's my favorite lollipop.

"Damn, Juno." He bucks forward, the tip of his dick hitting the back of my throat.

I continue my pace, cranking up the speed little by little, and he groans like a game of hot and cold, telling me how close we're getting to him coming. When his hands tug on my hair, he's hit his threshold and I work him as I have the past few days, the way I know will get him off.

"I'm gonna come," he says and bucks again in my mouth.

The bell on my door rings and Colton freezes as his cum leaks into my mouth as if it's an afterthought.

"Colton," his mom says with a chuckle. "Are you the matchmaker now?"

"Mom," Colton says and coughs.

He glances down between his legs and my mind scrambles with a million half-assed ways to get out of this. I could've dropped a pen, but why would Colton be tucked into the open space in my desk instead of helping me? Nothing explains why I'm down here except that I was just blowing her son.

My head falls against his kneecap and I want to cry from embarrassment.

"Where's Juno? I brought her this cute knick-knack I found at the flea market in Greywall this weekend. Isn't it cute? It says, 'Trust me, I'm a matchmaker.'"

"Yeah. Cute."

"So, where is she?"

Colton laughs because he always laughs when he's uncomfortable. I punch his thigh, which only makes him laugh harder.

"She's looking for something," he says.

"Where?"

Colton laughs harder now. "Okay, Mom, you know we're grown and everything, right?"

Oh no, he doesn't. My hand slides up his pant leg and I pinch any skin I can find.

"Ouch!" He wheels back and grabs his leg.

"What?" His mom sounds panicked because Colton, her only child, is her world. "Are you okay?"

"Yeah. I'm fine. I'm sure Juno will be back soon. Just leave it and I'll give it to her."

"Oh, I'll wait. Where'd she go?"

He slyly slides his hands under the desk, tucking himself into his boxers, but he has no choice but to leave his pants open if he doesn't want to tip her off as to where I am. "I'm not sure. The bank?"

To beg for money if that was the case.

"How are things with the two of you?" she asks.

I hear the vinyl of my guest chair crinkle, suggesting she's getting comfortable.

"Good."

"Good as in we'll be planning another wedding soon?"

I gag and Colton coughs to mask the noise.

"You're not getting sick, are you, sweetie?"

"No. Don't come over here. I'm not five, Mom, I don't have a fever." He waves her off before she can come over to this side of the desk and see his pants undone and me between his legs.

At least we've moved the conversation somewhere other than a wedding. Hello, it's been one week since he left his bride at the altar for me. What is she thinking?

"Are you sure? You know you sometimes get spring allergies."

"I'm positive."

I want to laugh out loud because he just said this morning he'd used up the last of his allergy pills and had to grab some today.

"Listen, Mom, I know she has to head out to Anchorage for a blind speed date thing. I don't know if she'll be coming back here before she leaves."

"When did she start doing that? She's always just been a matchmaker, not a dating service."

Leave it to Mrs. Stone to ask questions that will make Colton think harder about what I'm doing. Shit.

"I guess to get more customers. I'm not really sure," he says.

"Is she okay? You do know to not only talk about yourself in a relationship, right? You have to be a true partner and listen to her as well. It's a two-way street—"

Colton holds up his hand. "I know. No worries, you've taught me well."

And she has. You never have to worry about that with Colton, which is precisely why I don't want him to find out about my failing business. He'll put on his superhero cape. I don't need him swooping in to save me.

"If you say so." She's quiet for a moment. "I'm sad to miss her. I really wanted to hug her because I'm so happy the two of you are finally together."

Colton smiles at his mom. It's the one that says he agrees with her.

"Well, I guess I'll come back tomorrow. Give me a hug."

"No," Colton says.

"What?" Mrs. Stone sounds confused.

"I have to go to the bathroom. If I get up and hug you without going to the bathroom first, I might pee myself."

I bite his jeans to muffle my laugh. That's the best he could come up with?

"I've told you not to hold it. You'll get a urinary tract infection."

"Sorry, Mom."

I cover my mouth before I lose it and crack up under here.

"Uh huh. Okay, love you."

"Bye, Mom." He waves and I'm assuming she's at the door.

"I love you too. Juno, you can come out from under the desk now. Oh, young love. Reminds me of your father and me."

The door chime rings, and Colton slides out, buttoning and zipping his jeans.

My cheeks are red hot. "I can never face your mother again," I say, crawling into his lap.

He holds me tightly, kissing my neck. "She might be weirded out, but she's cool with it."

"That's just wrong. For your mom to know I was doing that."

His fingers run up my back to the back of my head. "And you are a master at that, I'm telling you."

I climb off his lap. "Don't you have to go to the bathroom?" I chuckle.

"What was I supposed to say?"

"How about you think you might be catching a cold?"

"You know that wouldn't stop my mom."

I nod. "True." I pick up the box. "Ready?"

"Yeah." He takes the box from my hands and the bell chimes again.

This time it's Earl, the mailman.

"Hey, Earl," Colton says. "Put it in the box."

Earl does and he nods at me. "Miss Juno. Mr. Colton. Congratulations are in order?"

Colton glances at me over his shoulder and back at Earl. "I guess."

"Happy to hear it. You make a lovely couple. Have a nice day."

"You too, Earl," we say in unison.

I go to the box and pick up the mail, then shove it into my drawer.

"You can open it on the way," Colton suggests.

"Nah. I'm sure there's nothing important." I wave him off.

Hopefully, he didn't see the red line on the paper through the envelope like I did. Of course if he did, he probably thought nothing of it, having never received a past due notice in his life.

Colton walks out to his truck that's parked along the side of the road. I look at the picture of Aunt Etta and debate if this whole matchmaker thing is even worth fighting for. Maybe my mom had it wrong and I can't predict who belongs together. The fact that my business is failing is a bigger sign than my red hair. The color means exactly what it did when I was eleven—that I'm different.

TWENTY-FIVE

Colton

As usual, Juno organizes the blind speed dating thing perfectly and her customers—who are most of Kingston's buddies—are happy. Thankfully, whether Stella got Juno's message or not, she didn't show up. Although I view the situation differently than Juno. Kingston deserves to know that Stella's back so he can clear things up with her. Figure out where they stand going forward, even if it's as acquaintances or nothing at all.

After everyone blindly talks through the partitions, a few of Kingston's buddies head into the bar area to mingle with girls, but Kingston heads my way, a beer in hand.

"What's up?" he says, sliding into the stool across from me.

"Nothing. No matches?" I ask.

He smirks and shakes his head. "I just can't. You know?

I've tried. You ever feel like you're filling a need and not the hole?"

I raise my eyebrows and he laughs.

"Yeah, I phrased that wrong. I guess I mean, I sleep with girls, but nothing really fills the void."

I tip my water bottle toward him. "There's a better word."

He chuckles.

Sadly, I do understand, and my gaze lingers on Juno talking to some of the ladies who didn't match with anyone. She hands them business cards and they continue talking, one of them pointing toward our table. I catch her eyes for a moment, and she smiles and turns back to the group, telling them something.

"I'd only tell you this, but I'm sick of wasting my time with the entire dating thing," Kingston says. "For a while I was cool with it, but now all my siblings are getting hitched and having babies."

"You're only twenty-five," I say, and he nods.

"I guess so." He glances over his shoulder. "I looked Stella up the other day. Being back at Cozy Cottage with Selene last week made the urge too strong to ignore."

My throat tightens. "And?"

"From what I can tell, she's still in New York. I'm thinking about going out to Sedona's, maybe pop in on Stella."

"Don't track her down," I say, mostly because he's wrong. Stella's literally minutes away from us right now and I hate that I'm keeping this secret.

"It's been a while. We were cordial at Austin and Holly's wedding. We friended each other on social media. That means something, right?"

Something I've noticed about Kingston is that he's

almost always willing to tell others his feelings. Where Rome and Denver always hid them, and I think Austin, being the oldest, felt like he had to keep it all in, Kingston wears his heart on his sleeve, so to speak. It's admirable.

"You're talking to a guy who waited for more than a decade for your sister to come to her senses."

He chuckles and sips his beer. "She's a slow learner."

"Excuse me." Juno slaps him on the back of the head. "You better not have been talking about me."

"It took you forever to admit your feelings for Colton."

Juno sticks out her tongue, weaving her way between my legs and wrapping her arms around my neck.

"Did you have to tell those girls I'm taken?" I ask.

She draws back and narrows her eyes. I nod toward the girls with the business card, and she laughs. "Sorry, Don Juan, they were interested in Kingston."

Kingston laughs.

"Ouch," I say.

"Ouch? You have the best girl in this place."

I tighten my arms around her and kiss her neck. "That's right. You are a brilliant matchmaker."

She giggles.

"Excuse me?" A woman approaches and I straighten, removing my lips from Juno's neck. "I had a few questions."

"Sure." Juno takes her to the side and pulls a business card from her back pocket.

Kingston and I strip our eyes off them and get back to our conversation.

"I have a question," I ask.

"What's up?"

"It's personal, and if you don't want to tell me, you don't have to, but can you afford the apartment by yourself?"

This isn't something I had intended to ask Kingston

before I asked Juno, but I saw the bills in her mail that Earl dropped off. Juno's too proud to admit that she might be struggling financially. My mom's right—why now, after all these years, is Juno running these blind speed dating nights?

Kingston's eyebrows rise. "You guys are rushing things."

"Don't tell your sister—you know how slow she prefers things to go—but I don't really see the sense of paying for two places when I intend for us to speed this up faster than a relationship that doesn't include over a decade of friendship."

He puts his hands in the air. "I'm not bringing it up to her, but yeah, I can afford it. Truth is though, I may just move out and get a place closer to Anchorage if she moves in with you."

"You'd leave Lake Starlight?"

He shrugs. That's where Kingston isn't like his siblings. Most have stayed in Lake Starlight. I think everyone views Sedona as just not coming home after college, but someday she'll return. And Phoenix goes back and forth between Los Angeles and Lake Starlight, but her home is here. Kingston is the one who never seems to be in Lake Starlight except to sleep.

"Well, don't say anything. I haven't asked her, and I'm prepared to get the brush-off at first."

Kingston sips his beer. "You don't get sick of her acting like that?"

I shrug. "I love her. To love someone, you love all the parts of them—their faults as well as their attributes. One day I hope I love her enough that she doesn't feel like she can't be all in. If I ever get her to marry me, then you'll know I broke her down."

He laughs and tips his bottle toward my water bottle. "You're the only man who can do it." He sips his beer. "Oh,

I was thinking, let's get everyone together for Jamison's game. They're playing the Seattle Sounders this weekend. I'm off unless I get called in."

"Yeah definitely, we can do it at my house."

"Perfect."

"*Bailey!*" one of his buddies calls.

Kingston holds up his hand. "I better go. They can get kind of rowdy and I don't want it to ruin Juno's chances of having these events here. Text me details." He stands and heads into the other room.

"Kingston," I call, and he turns around. "As much as it sucks, sometimes you have to move on with your life until that person is ready to face whatever it is between you."

"Is that how you got my sister? Pretended to get married to push her to make a move?" He laughs as if that's absurd, and although I smile, guilt pierces my gut.

"Be good, King!" Juno yells, waving and coming back to me. She puts her arms around my neck. "Ready to take me back to your house?"

"I didn't even give you a pickup line."

"Eh. Those are overrated. I am the angel God sent down to Earth. You don't need to walk by again because it was love at first sight, and I think I have a Band-Aid in my purse for that scrape on your knee from falling for me." She kisses my lips. "See, I took care of it, so now I can crash at your place, Microsoft." She winks.

I laugh, stand, and grab the box of her stuff, which I carry out the back door.

On the way home, the guilt over what Kingston said grows, making me feel sick to my stomach, and I clench her hand. "Juno?"

"Yeah." She looks up from her phone.

"How long did you know you had feelings for me?"

She tucks her cell phone inside her purse. "I think they were always there... just... you know how messed up I can be about the future."

I nod. She didn't decide where she was going to college until April. She hates to make any future commitments, and the fact Kingston is aware of it says she's been like that for a long time. Maybe even before her parents' death, but for some reason, I associate the two as intertwined. We were too young when her parents died to know for certain.

"But the good thing is I did." She leans over and kisses my cheek.

"It wasn't only because I was about to marry Brigette though, right?"

She turns down the radio and faces me so her back is pressed to the window. "What's going on?"

I should've figured she'd read me. It's the number one problem of knowing each other as long as we have. We've witnessed the other in too many circumstances. It's like being a married couple without the sex.

"When I agreed to marry Brigette, I was upset. You had just told me about Trey, and I was pissed off that you'd slept with him and not me. I may have agreed to marry her out of spite." There. It's all out there. She can get mad if she chooses, but I would have never been able to continue without her knowing the truth. That I'm not the selfless guy she thinks I am.

"I figured. I don't like it, but I'm glad to be where we are now. I hate myself for doing that, hurting you so much for so long."

I stop at a light and now I can finally look at her. She's really not mad. At least she doesn't have that scowl I associate with her being pissed off. "You're okay with that?"

She shrugs. "I see it as the past. After you told me, I

connected all the dots. I was so scared of losing you, it took me actually losing you to make me act. As sad as that is."

The light turns green and I press on the gas to get us home. "Thanks for understanding. I'm sorry if you felt I tricked you in some way. I would never want our relationship to start like that."

She squeezes my hand. "Colton Stone, I've known you long enough to know you don't do mean-spirited things."

I nod and pull into my driveway. "Have you thought about moving some stuff in?"

She opens up the door. "Not yet. It's only been a week. Slow the train a little." She laughs, getting down, and disappears into my house.

Her phone dings and I pick it up from the center console. It's an email alert and her screen lights up, popping up the thread. I glance at the garage door into the house and click on the message from her landlord. He states that he cannot give her any more time. The rent is due by this Friday; otherwise he'll be closing her office Saturday.

My head falls back to the headrest and I close my eyes. How did I not see she was in trouble before now?

I turn off her phone and pull out mine, messaging Mario to find out the stipulations of my loan and do I have to use it for Four Paws.

TWENTY-SIX

Juno

Friday morning, I knock on Grandma Dori's apartment door in Northern Lights Assisted Living and wait for her to answer. Going to her is really a Hail Mary. I hate asking her for money.

"Juno," she says when she opens the door, her bluish-tinted hair in curlers. "Come in."

I walk in to see a hairdresser from Clip and Dish cleaning up some things in Grandma's kitchen sink.

"Since when do you not go to the salon?" I ask, and the hairdresser smiles at me.

"Mila didn't mind coming here this time. Something is up with my knee." She sits down on the couch, massaging it.

My entire life, I've never seen Grandma even sick. The woman is unstoppable. "Are you okay?"

She waves off my concern. "Stop it. Why are you here?"

I know Grandma Dori has some money, but I cannot just take her money to save a company I'm not sure I love anymore. I change my mind—I won't even ask. "Just wanted to say hi."

"Hmm... what's the real reason?" I glance back at Mila at the kitchen sink, and Grandma follows my movements. "Mila, you should go to the cafeteria and get some of the custard they have today. If anyone gives you trouble, you tell them you're my girl."

Mila either takes the hint or she loves custard because Grandma's door shuts a minute later.

"What's really going on, sweetie?" Grandma asks me, and I release a breath.

"Do you think Aunt Etta is real?"

"You mean did your mother make her up?"

I nod.

"Why would your mom do that?"

"Because I was an eleven-year-old who felt like I didn't belong. Because my siblings were making fun of me, as were the kids at school. Hank Billings told me they bought me at a pawn shop on one of Mom's trips."

"The Billings are assholes, you know that."

I nod. "I'm just not sure I'm really matchmaker material."

Her eyes narrow. "Why on Earth would you think that? You've never once doubted yourself. Why now? Especially when your own love life is going so well."

I smile, thinking about Colton. I should never have waited as long as I did to face how I feel about him. Although the fear that I'm going to lose him still lives just beneath that layer of love, I've done a really good job of pushing it as far down as I can. "I don't know. I'm just wondering."

"First of all, that's your mom's family, so I only really know what your mom told you and whatever you dug up."

"Etta could be some random picture that means nothing, and I've clung to this belief my entire life for what? To feel like I somehow belong to my siblings even if I don't look like them?"

"Look like them? Have you seen Holly?"

Has she really gotten so old she doesn't remember who is actually her actual grandchild?

"Holly isn't blood," I say.

Grandma waves me off like she does when she knows someone else is right, but she's older and wiser and we should just believe her. "The only ones who actually look alike are Phoenix and Sedona and Rome and Denver. The rest of you all—"

"Brooklyn and Savannah are both blonde."

"Well, what about Austin? He doesn't look like anyone."

"He looks like his brothers. I have this red hair."

"Well, sweetie, I'd describe your hair more as auburn with some dark undercurrents. Not to mention, what does hair color really prove?"

"It's also my pale skin. No one has pale skin like me."

"All of these silly things could be solved with hair dye and a fake tan. I was there when you were born, Juno. You're a Bailey."

I sulk in the chair. "I didn't really believe Hank Billings. I didn't think I was bought at a pawn shop or flea market." I shrug. "I just feel like I've put all my rocks into being a matchmaker and what if Mom lied to me?"

"Did you know your mother to be a liar?"

"No, but I only knew her for thirteen years."

Knock, knock.

"Perfect timing. Get the door."

I stand and open the door to find Savannah there with a stroller.

"Brinley," I say, bending to stare into the stroller at my beautiful niece.

"You wake her and you're dead." Savannah pushes the stroller into the apartment. "You're getting your hair done, Grandma? I'm not sure Brinley should be exposed to those fumes."

"It's not a perm, they're just rollers," Grandma Dori scolds. We all seem to be on our last nerve today. "Do you think I didn't raise a child of my own?"

"What are you doing here?" Savannah asks me.

"I could ask you the same thing," I say.

"Because I have to talk to Grandma about business." She moves the stroller back and forth to keep Brinley asleep. "How's things with Colton, you little vixen?"

I feel heat fill my cheeks. "Fine."

"Juno's back to her whole 'she's not a real Bailey' thing again," Grandma Dori says.

Savannah scoffs. "Juno, you're a Bailey."

"I know I'm a Bailey, but I'm not sure if I'm a matchmaker. Did Mom ever lie to you?"

Savannah laughs. "And I thought I was hormonal. I went from mean to nice and now I'm in some weird galaxy where I cry about her getting older and yell at Liam for putting the lotion in the wrong place."

"That's motherhood," Grandma Dori says, cool and calm.

"Juno, you need to relax. You're good at what you do. This person at my work still refers you out because you got her brother with someone. They're married and have, like, a trillion kids. Which after one, I'm not sure why people have more." She looks at Brinley and smiles. "Although when she's sleeping, she's beautiful."

I laugh. "Have you always loved working at Bailey Timber?"

She balks. "You're joking, right? No. Remember a few years ago when Holly's dad's business was threatening ours and I thought we were going down? That was bad…" Her eyes laser in on mine as if she can see what's really wrong. She glances at Grandma and back at me. "Call me later," Savannah whispers.

"I better go anyway. If I can't hold my niece, then I'm outta here." I give Grandma a kiss on the cheek. "FYI, Colton wants his key back and Ethel is creeping him out."

Grandma Dori laughs.

"What am I missing?" Savannah asks.

"Grandma used a key to get into Colton's house the morning after the wedding."

"Ew, why would you do that? You want to see them going at it?" Savannah's face is one of pure disgust.

"And Ethel looks at him like he's her next social security check," I say.

"She does not and so what? You should feel complimented that she's admiring his body so much," Grandma says.

Savannah and I share the same look. Like one more word and we're going to run to the toilet.

"Tell Colton to get used to the key thing," Savannah says. "The other day I thought Brinley was missing when I went to her crib to get her only to find Grandma Dori with her in the family room."

Grandma laughs.

"It's not funny. I thought someone had kidnapped my child!"

"And then Liam came running out in his boxers. Ethel had no idea he had that many tattoos." Grandma Dori's eyes light up and now I'm thoroughly grossed out.

"Why is Ethel always with you anyway?" Savannah asks.

"Because the sheriff said if he found me driving, he'd put me in jail. I think he's blowing smoke, but with Ethel's family in Sunset Bay it's like she's part of ours."

I kiss Savannah on the cheek. "Bye."

"Wait up," Savannah says before she points at Grandma. "Do not wake her up. I have to talk to you, and I'm not doing it while you're cooing at Brinley."

The two of us step out into the hallway.

"Is SparkFinder not doing too well financially?" Sav asks.

"Why would you ask that?"

"Because that's usually when the love for something dies. When you're doing things like blind speed dating in a bar to make money instead of why you got into match-making in the first place, it tells me something is going on."

"How do..." It doesn't matter how she heard about the work I'm doing in Anchorage. Silly me, I thought all my siblings who just had babies were in lala land. I guess not. "I'm fine."

"You'd tell me, right?"

"Of course." I nod.

"No, you wouldn't, but I have to go in there to rescue my baby because I just know Grandma's not going to listen to me. Come over one day and we can go over your books. Figure something out."

I turn and leave, only to hear Savannah open the door and yell, "I told you not to wake her!" And then Brinley screams.

I smile to myself. I left at the perfect time.

Driving back to my office, I think about Savannah's words of advice. She runs a huge company. Maybe she could've helped me, but it's Friday and Mr. Richards wants his money for last month and this month's rent and I don't have it, so I'm going to have to get my things out.

I park down the block, and I'm surprised to find Colton waiting at my office door.

He holds up a bag from the sandwich place in Sunset Bay. "Lunch for my girl."

"Sunset Bay?"

"Had to go to deliver puppies."

"Did you bring one back with you?" I open the door to my office, and he follows me inside.

"Is that something you'd want?" He places the bag on my desk and pulls out the sandwiches.

"I'm actually surprised you don't already have one."

He nods. "I never felt settled enough for one, but now…" He wraps his arms around me and kisses my lips. "If my girlfriend wants one, I want to make her happy."

"Oh, would you? Well, maybe it's something we should talk about."

"First you need to move in." He squares his eyes on me.

I blow out a breath and wiggle out of his hold. "I'm starving. Tell me you got me the bacon turkey ranch?"

He stands in the middle of the room, apparently unwilling to answer me or move.

I look at him. "What?"

"Stop dodging the topic. Why won't you move in with me?"

"What about Kingston?" Kingston actually told me a few nights ago, when I stopped home to grab some clothes, he's thinking about moving closer to Anchorage.

"Fine, Kingston can move in too. We have two extra bedrooms." He walks over and unwraps his sandwich.

"You mean *you* have two extra bedrooms."

He leans over my desk, and right before he takes a bite of his sandwich, he says, "What's mine is yours."

"We're not married," I say, opening up my sandwich, which smells delicious. Cheese gushes out of the side and I lick my lips in anticipation. We found this place on a whim during one of the first days of spring outings.

"Yet."

"Colton." I sigh.

"Juno," he mimics.

"I'm serious. We just got together. Let's enjoy this. What if..."

"I hate your what-ifs," he mumbles and bites his sandwich.

"What?"

He finishes chewing and digs paperwork out of his bag. "Forget it. We have something else to talk about anyway. I did something, and I don't want you to say no right away. I want you to listen to my argument."

He tosses some papers on my desk and I read the first line, realizing Savannah and Mrs. Stone aren't the only ones to figure out I'm a failure.

LOAN AGREEMENT

AS I SCAN THE DOCUMENT, there's no mention of Four Paws, but there is a loan amount issued to Colton Stone personally. I inhale, trying not to let anger take over, but you know what they say about redheads—we're fiery.

TWENTY-SEVEN

Colton

I wasn't going to present the loan to her in this way, but she pissed me off with her what-ifs. Why the hell can't she just move in with me? Hell, I'll take her brother too. Rent-free if he wants. I just want *her*. But I'm starting to realize I may have gotten her out of her desperation to not see me with someone else, but I don't truly have her because she doesn't want to think about our future.

"I'm not accepting this." She hands the papers back to me.

When I refuse to take my hands off my sandwich, she tosses the loan docs on top of the sandwich wrappers, dousing them with mayonnaise and seasoning.

"Damn it," I say, picking them up with one hand. "I know you're not making your bills."

She finishes chewing her bite and narrows her eyes at me. "It's none of your business."

"Yes, it is. You're my girlfriend and I want to help you."

"Is that loan big enough for Four Paws too?"

"No." I lean back in my chair. "I don't have enough collateral. It's strictly for you and SparkFinder, but I'm talking to Dr. Murphy next week when he returns from Portland. I'm sure we can figure out an arrangement."

"How do you know he won't find someone else?" She crosses her arms. She's dressed down today in a pair of leggings and a top that covers that ass I love.

"There is no one else."

"He could find someone. It's a vet business in a small town with no competition. Call the bank and tell them you want to apply for a business loan, not a personal loan."

"No."

"Damn you, Colton." She smacks her desk with an open palm. "Why?"

"Because you deserve it. Because you love being a matchmaker and I don't want to see your dream die."

She looks up. "And it's okay that your dream dies?"

I shrug. "My dream is just postponed. Not dead."

She stands and paces in front of her desk. "How did you know?"

"I saw an email and the past-dues when Earl dropped off the mail. The real question is why didn't you tell me?" It feels like a knife in the heart. Are we going to spend our entire life like this, where she doesn't tell me what's bothering her? "I'm supposed to be your confidant."

She throws her hands in the air. "We've been dating a week."

I throw my arms in the air. "We've been best friends since we were six."

Her eyes narrow. "Cute, Colton."

"I thought so." I sit smugly in my chair, my own sandwich untouched now. "Why do you keep everything inside? I don't understand."

She walks over to the picture of her Aunt Etta—or should I say shrine, because although it's only a picture, Juno looks at it as if Etta's her savior.

"I'm not sure I want to be a matchmaker and because of that..." She turns around and crosses her arms. "I'm closing SparkFinder. I won't accept your loan. Use it to fulfill your dream."

"What?" What the hell does she mean she's closing up shop?

She shakes her head. "My decision is made. I'm going to continue to do the blind speed dating because I have to earn a living."

"Are you sure?" She nods, walking back over to her desk, but before she can bypass me, I grab her wrist and tug her into my lap. "I love you."

She nods. "I know you do, but you can't be my savior."

"I'm not doing this just because we're a couple."

"I know. You would've done this just because of our friendship, but at some point, I have to find myself. And truthfully, my mind is a clusterfuck right now." I hold her tight and she lays her head on my shoulder. "I've never really thought of doing anything besides matchmaking. When I was younger, I felt it was my calling after my mom told me about my Aunt Etta. But I never really considered whether this is what I *want* to do with the rest of my life. I just did it. It's not a surprise that I never thought to improve or change things up to gain more clients because I was just living day by day. I didn't have any long-term goals for my business. And I'm sorry that it upsets you that I don't want to move in with you right now."

"Why don't you? Do you not see me in your future?" I hold my breath, waiting for her answer.

She picks up her head and cradles my face. "You're the one thing I know I want in my future. I'm scared I'm going to mess it up, but I can't help thinking about the what-ifs. What if as soon as I'm all in, you leave?"

I tilt my head, waiting for her to give me more to go on, but she doesn't. "Juno, I'd never leave you."

She presses her finger to my lips. "I'm not saying you'd do it willingly. Things happen."

I rear back and stare at her. Man, I had it pegged all wrong. She's not scared that I'm going to leave her—she's scared to rely on me because I'll die. Fuck.

I hug her, unable to say anything that might make it better.

MARIO CHANGES MY LOAN, and two weeks later, I'm signing papers with Dr. Murphy to be part owner of Four Paws.

There's no party to celebrate since I'm not making a huge deal about it in case I fail, but Juno's waiting for me at my house when I get there. I open up the garage door into my kitchen and my bag falls to the floor. She's sitting on the kitchen table, wearing a silk robe and—if my suspicions are correct—she's naked underneath.

"Are you the official part owner of Four Paws Veterinary Clinic, Dr. Stone?" she asks in a seductive voice, opening her legs to rest on the chair seat in front of her.

"I am. What's this?" I look around, not finding a candle, a flower, or even food. Not that I'm complaining if she's gonna be my meal.

"*Yay!*" She jumps off the table and I catch her, my hands molding to her ass when she wraps her legs around my middle.

I run my hands down her bare ass. "You *are* naked under here."

"I am, but I need you to get naked too because I have a surprise for you." She unhooks her legs and falls down my body, her fingers unbuttoning my shirt before her feet hit the floor.

"What is it?"

"I said surprise. Since you wouldn't let me have a party for you, I figured we'd prepare a meal from a movie like we always love to do."

"Oh, which one did you have in mind? Something from *Chocolat?*"

She shakes her head and her fingers undo my belt, the button, then the zipper of my slacks before they puddle on the floor. She takes my hand once I'm only in my boxer briefs and sits me down in front of the fridge.

"*9 ½ Weeks?*" My eyes widen and I smile.

She opens up her robe slightly and I get a glimpse of her shaved pussy. My dick salutes her and this kinky idea. "I did have to watch some of the movie by myself."

"I wanted to watch it with you." I tug her down to my lap and she squirms free, kneeling in front of me.

"Okay, close your eyes," she says, opening up the fridge.

"This is very bad for electricity."

She laughs. "You're a vet. You can afford it. Don't make me blindfold you."

I close my eyes as the cool air from the fridge flows out, hitting my nipples.

She puts something in front of my mouth, pushing it against my lips then retracting it. Finally, I chomp down and find it's a black olive. I chew it and swallow, waiting as I hear metal against metal.

"Open up, baby," she whispers.

I open for her to put a spoon in my mouth—filled with cherries from a jar. The sweetness hits my tongue and I moan. "I'd like to lick that off you later."

"That can definitely be arranged." She runs something cold over my lips.

I bite a strawberry and I open my eyes just a little when I hear her chewing.

"No peeking," she says, trying to hide what she's put into the fridge.

"I think the wrong person is being teased with food, don't you?" I get up and position her on the floor. "You close your eyes now."

"You're ruining my surprise." She semi pouts.

"Believe me, feeding you and watching you is a damn good present." I spot the glass of champagne already poured in the fridge, so I take it and tilt the glass to her lips. She swallows, but I over-tilt it so I can watch the champagne fall out of her mouth, down her chin, to her chest. Seeing an opportunity, I lick in the opening of her robe in the valley of her breasts.

"You're not supposed to touch me. You're breaking the rules, Stone."

I laugh, grabbing a piece of pasta salad. "Did you make this pasta salad?"

"It doesn't matter."

"Tell me."

"No," she says. I dangle it over her lips, teasing the Italian dressing on the seam of her lips. "That's probably why it's so good."

We both laugh. "Were you really going to make me bite a jalapeño pepper?"

She giggles. "We have to be authentic to the movie."

"Open up then." I poke her lips with a pepper.

She actually bites down on it slowly. "I can handle a little heat."

But her face scrunches in pain and she shakes her head, spitting it out. I tip the glass of milk to her lips, and just like the movie, it seeps out around the sides of the glass and drenches the front of her, the silk robe now clinging to her erect nipples.

"Bad idea," she says.

Instead of giving her the Jell-O, I give her a spoon full of cherries from the jar and she licks her lips after she's done. I tip the glass of champagne, once again dripping it down her body.

She opens her eyes and I lower her to the kitchen floor, my hands sliding the now-soaked robe aside. I suck and lick the champagne off her body.

"This is nice," she says, holding my head loosely, allowing me to venture over every inch of her body, cherishing and worshipping it.

When I reach her navel, she sits up and pours the bottle of champagne over my chest before licking it off me. Her small body is on mine, her center grinding along my length, teasing me.

"Congratulations, Doctor," she says, her lips at my neck and her teeth latching on to my earlobe. "You want your cake now?"

She straddles me and sits up. With her hands on my chest, I massage her ass and hips, continuing to rock her back and forth over my hard dick.

"I think I'm in the mood for pie."

She laughs, her head falling forward, but she stands, pulls my boxers down, then comes back over me and guides my cock to her entrance, sinking down my length. My hands mold to her breasts, tweaking her nipples as she rides me.

She's increasing the pace and I'm raising my hips to get as deep inside her as I can—when the door of my house opens.

"*Surprise!*"

"Fuck," Juno says, scrambling to get her robe, but our only choice is to hide behind the island, peeking over the top.

Within moments, Calista stands at the kitchen entrance with her eyes pinched together. Dion is playing with some electronic thing.

Phoebe points at the floor. "Cherry."

As if it can't get any worse, all the Baileys file in.

Denver laughs. "You kinky motherfu—"

Harley smacks him on the back of the head before he can finish.

Goddamn, I need that key back.

TWENTY-EIGHT

Juno

Downstairs, my entire family celebrates Colton buying Four Paws as we shower and try to rinse off our embarrassment. We're consenting adults, after all.

"Okay, babe, this is it. Operation get key back from Dori, okay?" Colton's serious, gripping my upper arms and staring me right in the eye.

"I'll try," I say.

Truthfully, I'm probably not as embarrassed as Colton. He's an only child. I'm one of nine. I'm used to the whole group walking in. I mean, Kingston found out what a tampon was used for when he walked in on me in the bathroom once. All of us were probably the first in our classes to know what the opposite sex's privates looked like. Denver's bare ass is practically branded in my brain.

"Try hard. I wasn't even able to finish, which means we'll be doing that fridge with the food thing again."

I kiss his lips. "I promise."

We walk downstairs, where my family has taken over Colton's house. Kingston has the television on, showing Jamison's soccer team. Everyone offers their congratulations to Colton, and they've spread out food from Wok For U. The kids are eating around the table and the women are in the kitchen, three of them with babies strapped to them. Phoenix has a glass of wine in hand, and I decide to join her.

Grandma Dori is with the kids, lecturing Calista about how just because she's a girl, it doesn't mean she can't hit someone back if they hit her first. Harley glances at them for a second but then shakes her head like she'll fix that later.

"This sucks," Harley says. "The whole reason I got pregnant was to be with you guys and now I'm pregnant alone again."

"Well, we still can't drink," Brooklyn says, nodding at my nephew strapped to her chest.

"Yeah, I'm not sure about this breastfeeding gig," Savannah says. "I mean, Liam's getting a little jealous and Brinley won't take a bottle. It's all me, and when I go back to work, I don't see this working."

Holly nods as though she gets it. "I can pump, but Easton eats all the time. I'm not even producing enough, so we already have to supplement with formula."

"You want to know what I can't stand? The fact that it's six weeks until you can have sex after you give birth and Wyatt acts like it's a life prison sentence. I don't even feel like having sex." Brooklyn shakes her head.

The other new moms nod as if they want to shout "amen."

I look at Phoenix and she widens her eyes at me. "So, sexy times in the kitchen, huh?"

Colton catches her words as he's grabbing a beer from the fridge. He rolls his eyes and shakes his head.

I say, "Yeah. I thought I said no party?"

"Grandma Dori already had it planned. I think because you're closing SparkFinder, she thought that you could use a party," Phoenix says.

"Are you okay?" Brooklyn's hand runs up and down on my arm.

"I'm good."

Savannah chews on her lip and looks around. I catch her and narrow my eyes.

"Liam." She tries to slide out behind Holly, but with the baby, she can't get away so fast.

I stop Savannah. "What's up?"

"Nothing." She shakes her head.

"Someone call Sedona, her man just scored a crazy goal," Kingston yells.

I stay in place with my hand on Savannah's arm. She has a secret.

"You'll find out tomorrow," she whispers.

"Tell me now."

"I can't," she says between gritted teeth.

"Is it bad?"

Her eyes flicker to Grandma, which means, yes, it's bad. "No. Not at all."

All the guys' cheering quiets in the other room.

"Oh shit. Get up, get up," Kingston says in a quieter voice, more like he's talking to himself.

All of our heads turn. Kingston and Denver are on either side of the television, both with their hands at their mouths.

"What happened?" Grandma Dori stands and leaves the children to see.

They replay the play and you see a guy come in to block Jamison's shot, hitting his leg from the side. We all watch as Jamison writhes in pain on the field. His teammates and the other team kneel around as the medical crew rushes out to him.

Phoenix slides by all of us, going to Griffin's side. They whisper together.

"Is Uncle Jamison hurt again?" Maverick asks Phoenix.

We all turn to him. Phoenix grabs him and holds him, whispering in his ear.

"The twins are keeping secrets!" Kingston yells, pointing at Phoenix.

She turns to Griffin and he shrugs. She releases Maverick, and he goes off to play video games with Dion.

"So, Jamison might have hurt himself a few weeks ago," Phoenix says. "They didn't think it was anything major. He took some time off to recover, and that's when Sedona came home for the shower. But I believe it's the same leg he hurt before."

We all turn toward the television and listen to the announcers, who are saying there was a rumor about him being hurt prior to this but that his team is known to be tight-lipped about injured players. The one guy analyzing the footage slows down the tape just as the other guy tries to block. You see Jamison go down, howling in pain.

"That's an injury that could end a career," the announcer says.

"I hope not, because Jamison's too talented of a player for his game to end this early. Plus New York doesn't stand a chance without him," the other announcer says.

We all look around and Phoenix is gone. I'm sure she's off to call Sedona. I really hope Sedona's okay. Jamison is carted off the field on a stretcher, grasping and hovering over his leg.

Colton comes over to me and puts his arm around my waist. "This is shitty timing, but I got the key," he whispers.

"Way to go, Magnum PI."

———

THE NEXT DAY is the official move-out date of my Spark-Finder office. I managed to make a deal with Mr. Richards, and since he didn't have anyone ready to move in, I got a few weeks to pack up my stuff. It's all going into Colton's garage until I figure things out.

"What else do you have?" Colton comes in, all sweaty and delicious and manly looking.

"Um, just my desk, and the back room with the table and chairs."

He nods and Kingston follows him to the back room.

I follow them, asking Colton, "Are you sure you're cool with me leaving everything in your garage? I could get a storage locker or something. Maybe I should just sell it all."

Colton abandons the stack of chairs he was going to take out and kisses my lips. "That's ridiculous. I have enough room for you and your stuff too."

He's been on me about moving in, and I'll admit—I'm at his house so much, it's kind of stupid that I don't. But at the same time, I can't pay half that mortgage right now and I don't want to be a freeloading girlfriend.

"Let's just handle this first," I say.

Savannah calls from the bathroom, "All clean. I'd like to see if Mr. Richards has anything to say about it."

"Thanks."

She rubs my arm with her palm. "Are you sure you want to do this? I can give you money. A loan if you'd like."

I shake my head. "Absolutely not."

She nods because we're cut from the same cloth. She wouldn't accept help either if our roles were reversed.

We follow Colton and Kingston out of the office to the truck outside, but another truck, a pink truck, honks while coming down the road.

"I'm so sorry," Savannah whispers as we watch it come to a stop behind the moving truck.

"Is this what you were keeping from me?"

She nods.

Liam walks up the sidewalk, pushing Brinley in a stroller. "Thank goodness we didn't miss it, baby girl." Liam's enthusiasm says whatever this truck is supposed to be is making his day. "Tell Mommy how you pooped through two onesies today and she's on diaper duty for the rest of the day." Liam talks as if he's a baby himself.

"Daddy's wrong. Mommy has changed more diapers than Daddy has in total." Savannah pretends to tickle Brinley.

"Please do not be one of those couples who pass on their passive-aggressive arguments through their kids," Kingston says.

Colton leans over to read the side of the truck before he looks at me. "Did you buy a truck?"

I point at myself. "Me? No. Why?"

The side door opens, and Rome slides open the side window like you would if someone were ordering food.

"Going into the food truck business, Rome?" I ask.

He shakes his head and bites down his laugh.

Calista jumps down with Dion. "*Yay*! That was so

much fun." She grabs my hand, dragging me over to the truck.

"Oh my God," I say.

"Isn't it great?" Grandma Dori files out with Ethel right behind her. "Thank Rome for his connections. I paid for the paint job. No repayment necessary. It's just for you being such a great granddaughter." She pinches my chin.

It's a food truck, painted in pink with SparkFinder on the side.

"I figured this way you go to them," Grandma says. "You can travel. Maybe do fairs and stuff."

I glance back at Colton, who's covering his mouth to hide his laughter. Grandma Dori is so happy and proud of herself.

"Um... thank you?" I say, opening my arms and hugging her.

"Well, go. Get in and drive it around. Rome will show you the ropes on how to use all the little gadgets."

"And maybe you could bake some heart-shaped cookies or snacks for your customers because it has a working kitchen," Ethel adds.

I smile at her, but she's busy staring at Colton.

"Well, let me finish up here." I look toward the practically vacant office now.

"I can finish up, babe. You go," Colton says, and I narrow my eyes at him.

"Okay, let's do this," Rome says.

I give him the death stare he deserves for being a part of this whole thing.

"I'll stay here with Colton," Ethel says.

Colton smiles but steps to the left, away from her. Ha! Serves him right.

Once I'm in the truck, Rome tells me where to insert the key. We drive around the square of downtown Lake Starlight, and Grandma keeps leaning over to beep the horn at everyone as if we're in a parade. My cheeks grow hotter and hotter the more attention we gain.

"Now park on the corner right there and I'll show you how to open up the outside while the kids play at the park," Rome directs me, and I park. It's surprisingly easy to maneuver.

We go out, and thankfully Grandma goes to the park with the kids.

When she's out of earshot, I say, "I can't believe you entertained this idea with her."

He laughs. "What did you want me to do?"

"Not get me a food truck and allow her to paint it with my logo. I mean, who is going to go to a matchmaker in a truck?"

He shrugs. "I've never understood why people go to a matchmaker at all, but they do. I agree with G'Ma D—this is good for you. No overhead cost, and you know what? Your first gig, I'll supply some appetizers."

"No doubt with your business cards," I say.

"Hey, I scratch your back, you scratch mine. Welcome to small business."

"Rome!" I bury my head in my hands and sit on the back of the truck. "I'm such a failure. This is just pathetic."

He sits next to me and wraps his arm around me. "I know it's hard to be closing your shop, but explore the opportunities this can give you. You might find something you love about it. I wasn't crazy about Dion at first, but he's grown on me."

I elbow him in the ribs, laughing.

"Yeah, I know, that kid's had me before he peed in my face during his first diaper change."

I sit up and swipe the tears from my eyes. "Thanks for this. I do appreciate it."

He nods. "Anything for my little sister."

TWENTY-NINE

Colton

It's been five months since Juno closed up SparkFinder and she still hasn't moved in with me. I don't bring it up much anymore, but all that changes today. I've given her enough time to get used to us.

She's actually enjoying the matchmaking delivery truck, driving it to some small town fairs where she conducts blind speed dating. Mostly, the fact she's parking it helps her gain some business. She does love matchmaking and I'm determined to prove it to her. I've even put something together on my computer to prove it to her.

But that surprise is for later. For now, I'm hiding up in the treehouse in the Bailey backyard—where I've been for at least twenty minutes—when I hear the voice I've been waiting for.

"You sure you want to play in the treehouse?" Juno asks

Calista, my little helper. "Aren't you cold? Shouldn't you be wearing a coat?"

"Nope. I'm fine. Alaskans have thick blood, right?"

"I suppose so," Juno says. "Where are Dion and Phoebe?"

"Oh, this is my day to help Uncle Austin and Aunt Holly. I get to come over here and help with baby Easton all by myself."

"Really? I didn't know that. Do you help Aunt Brooklyn and Aunt Savannah too?"

"No. Only Aunt Holly."

"Interesting."

In truth, Calista is here because Juno told me she was coming here today and I'm using Calista to get my plan in motion. I've had the idea for a long time, but I wanted to make sure it was a surprise and limit the number of Baileys included because this is just for us.

"Oh, I have to go to the bathroom." I hope Calista becomes an actress, because she's born for it. "I'll be right back. You go up."

"I can wait," Juno says.

"No. I'll be a few minutes. It's number two. You go."

I stifle a chuckle. This is the chancy part of the plan, but if I know Juno as well as I think I do, she'll come up here just to reminisce before Calista comes back.

Just as I thought, Juno climbs the ladder while I peek out the window and watch Calista run back to the house.

My heart feels as if it's beating in my throat. This is the moment. Our moment to take our future in our hands.

Her head pops up. "Colton?" She scrunches her forehead. "I thought you were working?"

Then she looks around at the twinkle lights and the pictures hanging off the cords I strung around the inside perimeter of the treehouse. Us at six in the sandbox at my house—the first playdate our moms had together. At seven, when we went to the fair in town and got to ride the Tilt-A-Whirl. At eight, when our families went camping together and we were out in a canoe in the middle of the lake by ourselves and our dads had to come fetch us because we ventured out too far. All the way up to sixteen when we got our licenses, our high school graduations, my college graduation. And there's an entire wall of the treehouse dedicated to the last six months when we became more than just best friends.

"Colton." She sighs, her hand at her mouth as she soaks up all the memories. "We were so young." Her fingers graze a picture of when we were nine, learning to ride quads.

Then she spots the box in my hand and I fall to bended knee.

"No, Colton." She shakes her head, looking a little frantic.

"Yes, it's time. I know you're scared, but I'm here and I'll always catch you. Make all my dreams come true and do me the honor of being my wife? Will you marry me, Juno?"

She smiles and her hand runs along my cheek. A move she does when I've pleaded a good case. She did it right before agreeing to *leave* a few things at my house in a drawer. Or when I bought her a toothbrush to keep at my house.

Then she looks at the worn floorboards and the smile strips from her face and her hand leaves my skin. "I'm sorry, Colton, I can't." She shuts the ring box.

"What?" All the breath leaves my body.

"We're happy, aren't we? We don't need rings and a legal piece of paper."

"I do," I say, anger growing inside me.

"Why?" she asks innocently, as if it's an everyday question.

"Because I want us to build a life, and for me, that includes a wife. Not a girlfriend. Not a live-in roommate. Actually." My eyes go wide. "I don't even have a live-in roommate because you won't move in with me."

"I told you. It's hard for me. I don't want to lose you. I don't want something to happen to you."

"Nothing is going to happen to me because you marry me. Why do you think just because I'm in your life and you're happy, something bad is going to happen?"

She stares at her hands. "Can we please just go back to the way things have been? We're happy. Why mess that up?"

"Because we can be happier. Because we can commit our futures to one another."

"I am committed to you."

I shake my head, the crease between my eyebrows deepening. "You're not."

"I am. You can't say I'm not." Her voice rises to match mine. "Not wanting a marriage says nothing about my commitment."

"To me it does. I get that there are couples out there who don't care about the piece of paper or shared names, and that's great for them. They got what they wanted. But I want a wife. I want a Mrs. Stone. I want my kids and my wife to share the same name as me. I want to promise to the entire world that I will cherish you all the days of my life. I want us to sleep in the same bed every night."

"We do sleep in the same bed every night."

I shove the ring box in my pocket. "You have to be fucking kidding me. I gotta go."

"Don't leave." She grabs my arm, but I go around her, climbing down the ladder.

I stop when I'm chest level with the floorboards. "Just so you know, when you want to blame someone for us not working out, look in the mirror, Juno. Look in the mirror."

I climb the rest of the way down the ladder and walk around the side of the house.

Austin meets me on the other side of the garage with Easton strapped to his chest. He probably heard me.

"Hey, Colt," he says, reaching for my arm. "Let's just talk this out. Let me speak with her. She loves you. I know she does."

I turn around and toss him the ring box before climbing into my truck. "Tell Juno she can get her stuff out of my house because I'll be gone for the rest of the weekend."

"No. Don't go saying something like that because you're angry." Austin follows me. "Come on, you're like a brother to me. Let me just give Easton to Holly and we can talk."

"I can't. I gotta get out of here." I start the truck.

He backs away because of the loud noise. I see him soothing Easton and I feel bad, but I have to get as far as I can from Juno and any of the Baileys.

THIRTY

Juno

I pull a picture off the string. It's the one of my parents with Colton and me at my birthday when I turned thirteen, just weeks before they died. We didn't have huge parties growing up, but we were all allowed to take one friend and go anywhere we wanted. I chose Colton and asked to go rafting. It's a picture of us all right before we got on.

My arm is slung over Colton's shoulders, my parents smiling with one hand on each of our shoulders. All of us in swimsuits with life preservers on.

I curl into a ball and hold the picture to my chest, crying because I desperately want to get over this fear. Doesn't Colton know that? Why won't he give me any more time?

"Juno Bailey!" Grandma Dori screams up to me from below. "I will not come up there, but you are getting your little tushy down here right now!"

I wipe my cheeks then peer down the hole, and sure enough, she's standing at the bottom of the ladder, glaring at me. "I'm not changing my mind. He's rushing me and I'm not ready."

"He's not rushing anything. The two of you have been friends since you were six. If anything, he's going too slow. I told him not to accommodate you, that you had to face reality."

"That's nice grandma, tell him to push me to limits I'm not ready for."

"Ugh." She turns toward the house. "I'm going up, Austin, call the paramedics if I fall and record this... Juno gets nothing if I fall and die. She's cut from my will for making me go up there."

I throw my hands in the air. "Don't come up, I'll come down."

"Too late now, missy. Make room for me."

I blow out a breath and slide to the back of the tree-house to give her room.

She comes up, huffing and puffing and scolds me with her eyes.

"I told you I'd come down," I grumble.

"Well, I'm here, aren't I?" She sits down and takes a few breaths. "You've always been my hardest one."

"Thanks for the compliment," I say.

"Oh, stop it with your dramatics."

I hear someone else coming up the ladder. I assume it's Austin, but rather than joining us, his hand slides two books across the floorboards.

"Are we sure this is still stable?" Grandma tests the weight where she's sitting and picks up the books.

"I'm sorry, okay? I do love him, but he's rushing me into moving in together and now marriage. We've only been together for, like, six months." I pull my legs up to my chest and wrap my arms around them.

"This isn't about you and Colton. This is about you and an irrational fear. You'd think I'd have it easy and all of you would be wounded in the same way after your parents died, but no, each of you are so different. You came out thinking that the more you need someone, the more likely they'll be stripped away from you."

"That's not true," I say.

She gives me her bored look. The one that says she's the wise woman, listen to her. "Because you had Colton, I left you alone growing up. I didn't pry too much because I naively thought you were open and honest with him about your struggles. That you told him your fears and worries. I see now I was wrong." She points at me. "And you can put that in the books because I rarely admit when I'm wrong."

I make a checkmark in the air.

She scowls. "It wasn't until you came to my apartment all those months ago that I realized you were lost. That you didn't have your head on your shoulders like I thought."

"Is this supposed to be an uplifting conversation?"

"Let me get to my point."

I hold up my hands, telling her to go ahead.

"Weeks later, you were closing your business. I thought that's where your doubt in yourself came from. Because you kept asking if your mom would lie to make you feel like you belong. So I did some research." She opens one of the books. There's a tree with names on it. "I had both sides of your genealogy done, and to my surprise, your red hair comes from our side too."

"Really? You did this?" I lean in to see the book better.

She shoos me with her hand because we both know it was probably Mr. Miller at Northern Lights who did this for her. He's always asking me where my red hair came from. He says it's rare and he loves to trace down recessive traits with his genealogy hobby.

"It turns out that Aunt Etta was a redhead but look at all these Baileys with red hair too. And then I thought I remembered something, and I searched back to find some pictures. Sure enough, your grandpa was born a redhead, although it turned blond soon after as he grew up."

I pick up the book and look through the pages of all our ancestors. "You did all this to prove that my red hair is a Bailey trait too?" Tears well in my eyes.

"You've always been a Bailey. No other Bailey talks back to me the way you do. Who do you think you get that from? Yours truly." She thumbs at herself.

I swipe my eyes.

"And I had a matchmaker on my side too. A few generations ago and I'm not sure who she ever matched, but Mr. Miller found it." I laugh and she rolls her eyes because she slipped up by mentioning Mr. Miller.

"And the other book?" I ask, nodding toward it.

"Oh, well." She looks around the treehouse. "I'm not sure it's necessary after I see all these. Colton is one special guy." She picks up the book and hands it to me.

I open the first page, and it's filled with pictures of my siblings and me. There are none of my parents. There's Austin and Savannah helping us other five look into the two cribs of Sedona and Phoenix. There're more images of fights, huge fort builds, swimming in the lake, game nights, plays we put on.

"This is the best way I felt I could prove to you that you think you don't rely on anyone, don't let anyone get close in case you'll get hurt, but that's not true. You do." Grandma flips a few pages and there's more.

All of us at weddings, baby showers, new business openings. Rome there to give me that ridiculous matchmaking vehicle. Kingston there to help me move. Savannah cleaning the bathroom in my old office.

"They're my family, of course I love them. And they have to love me no matter what." I swipe another tear.

"Do they? Because up until five minutes ago, you thought you weren't related to them." She laughs. "If I ever see that Hank Billings, I'm going to give him a junk-punch."

I chuckle.

"I think you're missing the one other person who is at all these functions." She pushes the book closer to me.

"I know, I see how Holly joined, Wyatt—"

She shakes her head. "Look harder, Juno."

I look harder at the pages and smile because Colton's in every image. At Austin's wedding, he's in the background, helping to pass out wedding programs. He's helping Wyatt build the deck on his and Brooklyn's new house. He stands by my side as we watch Rome cut the ribbon at the opening of Terra and Mare. And it goes on and on. Colton always there, always present, always by my side.

"You've already been leaning on him and him leaning on you. Nothing's going to change that just because you wear a ring and you hold his last name. Although I do think Colton Bailey has a nice ring to it."

We both laugh.

"I wish I could promise you that nothing bad will happen. All of you deserve a lifetime of happiness, but life doesn't come with guarantees, Juno. But I can guarantee the universe won't conspire against you just because you're happy." She gives my hand a squeeze. "I have one question for you. Will it hurt any more or less if you lose him right now with your stubbornness than it will years from now when you're wearing his ring and living as his wife?"

I feel as if a band is growing tighter and tighter around my chest. "I'm just so afraid that if I'm too happy, something will happen to destroy it. Look what happened with Mom and Dad. They were so happy one minute and then they were gone."

Grandma Dori smiles, but sadness fills her eyes. "I hate to break it to you, but you don't have any control over that. No one does. All we can do is live our life." I lay my head on her shoulder, and she runs her fingers through my hair. "Life keeps happening to you whether you choose to live it or not, Juno, my strong one."

I burrow into her a little deeper. "I thought Savannah was the strong one?"

She laughs. "Savannah's hard-headed, for sure. But I see now that you've always kept up the façade of being strong, even though inside you needed someone to make you see it would all be okay. You and Savannah have something else in common too."

"What's that?"

"You both kept those boys away from you for so long. Had those arms locked out in front of you and would not bend to let them close."

I giggle.

"I'm serious. You were blessed to find love so young, and you both squandered it for years." She draws back and her finger lands under my chin, bringing my face up to look in her eyes. "My question is, how many more years are you going to lose by dodging fate?"

I shake my head. "It's too late. He hates me. If you saw how mad he was... he's never yelled at me like that. I hurt him."

"Well, I have no doubt you hurt him. All these pictures are proof of how long he's loved you. Lovesick puppy dog that he is. But you know Colton's not perfect. I wish he'd pushed you sooner. He's chased you his entire life. What do you think you should do now?"

The truth of her words hit me. "Chase him." I sit up straighter. "I have no idea where he is though."

"That's a nice excuse."

I pick up my phone and call him, but it goes right to voicemail. "I'm going to get him." I kiss her cheek. "Thanks, Grandma. Do you need help down?"

"You're welcome and no, you go. One of your siblings will help me."

I smile at her after stepping down one rung on the ladder. "We're so lucky to have you. You know that, right? We give you hell, but if we didn't have you, we never would've survived." Tears tumble down my cheeks and my vision grows blurry.

She pats my head. "I know, but it's nice to hear. You go now."

I nod and climb down the rest of the way.

"Now, Juno," she says.

I look up to the top of the ladder, my body buzzing to run. "Yeah?"

"You owe me one if you get him back. I expect Stella's phone number in return."

I shake my head and she smiles, although I don't think she's joking.

"Let me get him first." I run up the side of the house to the driveway until I reach my car.

"Juno!" Austin yells.

I turn around and he tosses me Colton's ring box. I catch it, confused as to why he has it. But instead of asking,

I say, "Thanks," slide into my car, and roar down the driveway.

I go way over the speed limit on the way to Colton's house, but when I get there, I find it empty. I run up the stairs and find the bedroom neat and orderly. Nothing out of place or out of the ordinary. Running back downstairs to the kitchen, there's no note, and when I check the garage, his truck isn't there. Where would he have gone?

I rush down the hallway to his office and don't see any clues. I sit at his desk and rub my temples before pulling out my phone to call Kingston, putting it on speaker.

"Heard you're in crisis," he answers.

"Seriously, how fast does the Bailey phone tree work?"

"You know the answer to that."

"Where would he go, King? He's not here, and I've blown it. He's finally reached his limit!"

"Whoa, whoa, whoa. Calm down first. You won't lose Colton. You're at his house, right? Is his suitcase there?"

"Hold on." I take the phone with me and rush upstairs where he keeps his luggage in the closet. "It's missing. Oh my God, he's flying somewhere."

"Boot up his computer. If he were home, let's hope he'd book a flight on his computer and not his phone."

I run back to the office and do as he says, entering Colton's password. "I don't see anything."

"Go to his history."

I scramble to click and finally find it. "There's nothing that sticks out to me."

"Go to his recent files on his computer. What has he been doing?"

"Okay." I scroll to his documents and click on recent activity. I click on the first one and it's a slideshow of pictures. "It's a picture slideshow of..." I lean forward. "No way."

"What is it? Please don't tell me if it's naked pictures of the two of you. I don't want that in my head."

"It's a slideshow of all my success stories with Spark-Finder. Pictures of them now, married or with kids. Each one thanking me. One of their kids is holding a sign that says, 'Juno the Matchmaker—if it wasn't for you, I wouldn't be here.'"

"Way to go, Colton," Kingston whispers.

"Oh, Kingston, they all look so happy and in love."

"And they found each other through you," Kingston says. "Still doubting that whole matchmaking thing?"

I click off the slideshow. "I need to find Colton right now. Where else do I look?"

"Let me see if he'll answer a call from me. I'll call you back."

"Okay, I'm going now to drive around."

"Just sit and wait. Maybe he'll return there."

"He took his suitcase. I'm going."

He blows out a breath. "Okay, I'll call you if he answers."

"Thanks."

We hang up and I grab my keys, going back to my car and thinking I'll drive to the airport. I press on the gas, and the streetlights pop on as the sky darkens. I try to call him again, but he doesn't answer. I hit the highway toward Anchorage with so much anxiety, I can't stop tapping my hand on the steering wheel.

A while later, my phone finally rings and it's Kingston. "Did he answer for you?"

"Juno, can you come and get me?"

"Where is he?" I ask.

"Just come and get me and I'll drive you to him."

"*Kingston!*" I yell.

"He's on his way up north to his parents' cabin."

My stomach sinks to the floorboards. "Wait." I pull over. "Did you talk to him?"

There's silence. "No, he didn't answer, but Mrs. Stone did."

"And what did she say?" I can barely get the words out, afraid of the answer. Do they know how stupid I've been? That I've jeopardized my future with their son?

"She said he called her and asked about the code. Told her he had to get away. Just come get me."

"Oh my God, King, she probably hates me." I can't get enough air in my lungs. It feels as if my throat is closing in. "I think I know my way there. If anyone asks, that's where I am."

"Juno, I'm not letting you to drive up there by yourself when it's almost dark. He's let me use the place a few times. I can get you up there, and I'll drive your car back. You can stay there and enjoy the makeup sex."

I cannot lose Colton because of my idiocy. I almost did once. I won't let it happen this time. "No, I don't have time to waste."

I click off and pull back on the interstate.

Ten miles down the road, I skid to a stop before I plow into the back of a semi-truck. Before I can breathe a sigh of relief, a car hits me from the back and I careen into the cement wall.

THIRTY-ONE

Colton

My mom texts me to say that the keycode is the same as it was the last time I was at the family cabin up north. She follows up to ask whether Juno and I are going together. I can't very well tell her Juno's coming because she'll see Juno around town. I have no choice but to tell her I need some time away and I'll call her tomorrow after I settle in. Surprisingly, she doesn't push me for more answers.

I turn up my music and turn off my Bluetooth.

My mind runs through the events since Juno and I got together. The last months, we've been happy. Juno was happy. I *know* she was. Sure, she didn't want to move in yet and I knew we'd have to take the wedding planning slow... but to actually say no to my proposal? It feels like maybe I don't know her anymore. Would she really throw all our happiness away because she's scared something bad will happen?

I understand losing her parents was hard on her. Hell, I understood why she constantly pushed away the possibility of us being more than friends. Her fear is real, and I respect that, but now I feel naïve that I thought she was over that fear.

My foot presses on the gas, eager to disappear before the embarrassment of Buzz Wheel reporting that Juno broke my heart hits the internet.

When a love song starts, I punch the button on the stereo, wanting anything other than a song that speaks to my feelings of heartbreak. Hell, I'll take opera over that.

I replay the conversation in my head, her words echoing in my ear. That she's committed to me. That she's happy living in limbo right now. And I think about how long it took to get her to admit her feelings for me in the first place. Maybe I am rushing her. Maybe I should've waited longer to propose. Let her get comfortable with us.

How can I forget the one thing Liam told me on that hill that dreary day in Lake Starlight fifteen years ago? That we have to be there for them. I've stuck by that with my friendship with Juno. Tried to be there for all of them in any way I could.

The day of Mr. and Mrs. Bailey's funeral comes back to my mind. Juno at thirteen with no tears pouring down her face.

Who am I kidding? She feels for me. Juno feels a lot. She just feels so deeply, it takes her time to come to terms with it.

I pull off the interstate only to pull right back on going the opposite direction, heading back to Lake Starlight. We'll figure this out, but we'll do it together. Not by me leaving her.

Miles away from Lake Starlight, traffic slows, and it isn't until after I've crawled along for five miles that I find out why. There's at least a fifty car pile-up in the northbound side. My hand instinctively goes for my phone to call Juno and let her know that I missed the accident and I'm okay—but then I realize she doesn't even know I was on this highway.

Traffic slows further as we creep past the blinking red and blue lights. The paramedics and firefighters run through the vehicles as smoke fills the air, metal sprinkled along the pavement. I notice a black truck parked close to the cement barrier on the other side.

I swear it's Kingston's truck. Once I get closer, I see the firefighter sticker on the back and I'm sure it's Kingston's. Why would he come out to the accident if he weren't on duty? Why else would his truck be here though? Maybe they needed to call more people in because of how many cars are involved?

The guy behind me honks his horn, but I don't care.

Kingston is running in one direction, stopping and waving over a paramedic.

I slam on my brakes, the guy behind me nearly rear-ending me. Instead of stopping, I pull off to the side of the road, park, and jump the barrier. Tell me that's not Juno's car. Please God, tell me that someone else has the same car. I run toward the car with my heart beating like a bass drum in my ears.

"Juno!" I yell.

Kingston looks up from talking to the driver and puts out his hands. "Colton, dude, you can't be here."

"Yes, I can. Is it her? Is Juno in that car?" I try to go

around him, but his hands are on my chest and he dodges every attempt. "Kingston."

He stops and nods. "She's gotta go to the hospital to get checked out. Meet us there. I'll keep you updated, okay?"

"Bailey, what the hell?" one of his firefighter friends says. I think his name is Lou. I've met him a few times. "It's your day off."

"It's my sister." He walks away from me, pointing at her car. "Her door is jammed."

"Shit. Okay." Lou follows Kingston's lead.

With their attention away from me, I run over to her car. Juno's head is bleeding, and her face is pale, but she's breathing. She's alive.

Thank God.

"Juno, are you okay?" I go to the door.

"Colton, out of the way," Kingston says, so I go around the car to the passenger side.

Lou uses a crowbar to pry open the door.

"I'm sorry. I never should've given you crap. If you don't want to marry me, that's fine. I'd rather just—"

Juno shakes her head, tears spilling down her face. Lou gets the door open, and Kingston undoes her seat belt.

"Slow, Juno," he says. "Let's wait for a stretcher."

She shakes her head. "I'm just a little shaken up. I'm fine." As she says it, her head lazily goes in a circle and falls to the headrest.

It's good to have connections because a paramedic comes over, fist-bumps Kingston, and they put Juno on a stretcher right away.

"Wait!" She tries to sit up. "I need my purse."

I snatch the purse and follow them to the ambulance. "I'm going with you."

"Your car?" Kingston points toward where I ditched my car.

"Tow it. I'm not leaving her again."

Juno smiles at me as we climb into the ambulance, Kingston saying he'll catch up with us.

As the paramedics do her vitals and make sure her injuries aren't worse, Juno points at her purse hanging off my arm. "Can I have that?"

"No, I got it. Just worry about letting them check you out." I grab her hand, thankful she's here and alive and talking to me. Forget marriage, I can deal with cohabitation common law marriage. As soon as I get her to move in, that is.

"Please, Colton, I need something." I hand it to her, and she smiles at the paramedic. "I swear, I'm good." She digs through her purse and hands me the ring box, tears in her eyes. "Ask me again."

"Juno," I whisper and shake my head.

"Ask me again." She nudges the box closer to me.

The paramedic smiles and stops working on her.

"If this is because you thought I was leaving, then don't. I'm not leaving. You're stuck with me regardless of whether you'll marry me or not."

She shakes her head. "No, I realized that I was an idiot and I was ruining our future because I was scared to lose you. But there's no difference. I love you, and if something bad happens, just because I'm not your wife doesn't mean my heartache would be less. I guess Grandma Dori is pretty damn wise. But don't ever tell her I said that."

A small smile tilts my lips. "So?"

She eyes the box in my hand. "Ask me again."

I remove the ring and hold it out. "Juno, will you—"

"Yes! I'll marry you!"

I laugh. The paramedic laughs.

Juno waves me over to her, where she wraps her arms around my neck and kisses me all over my face. "Forgive me for being so stupid?"

"I forgive you, but let me get the ring on your finger."

She pulls back, watching me take her left ringer finger and slide the round diamond with a silver band on her finger. She takes my head in her hands and rests her forehead to mine. "Do you think they'll feed us at the hospital?"

"You're hungry?"

"It was a very emotional day," she says.

AN HOUR LATER, she gets her release papers.

"You do realize you ruined my proposal?" I say as we walk out of the hospital room.

"Want to do it over again?"

Kingston turns the corner and smiles when he sees us in the hallway. "What's up? Glad to see it was only a minor injury."

I shake his hand. "Yeah, she's pretty lucky."

Kingston widens his stance, crossing his arms. "I have a question for you."

"Kingston, she needs her rest." I attempt to move us around him.

Kingston raises his one hand, ignoring me. "Before you guys go play doctor and nurse, I want to know why you were driving southbound?"

Juno looks at me. Now she knows I was coming back for her.

"Did you really think I could disappear without fighting for you?" I ask her.

She leans into me, pressing her cheek to my chest. "It's so unfair to all the women in the world that I get this guy. But I'm not trading him for anything." Juno hugs me tighter.

"You guys are getting sickeningly sweet," Kingston says.

"Get ready for those cavities then." Juno takes my hand and leads us down the hallway.

Kingston says he can take us out the ambulance way, so we don't have to go through the busy waiting room. Just as the doors open to the outside, a nurse comes out of the room to the right, losing her footing. Kingston grabs her arms to keep her from falling.

"Hey, thanks." The nurse looks Kingston up and down, clearly liking what she sees.

He nods and watches as she continues down the hall. We walk out the sliding doors, but Kingston stays inside. "I'll catch you two later."

"Bye, Kington," we say in unison, knowing what direction that situation is headed.

We walk toward my car.

"Why do you put up with me?" she asks.

I chuckle and kiss her temple. "It was never a choice. It's just always been you."

"Me what?" she asks.

"The one who lives in my dreams."

She stops us. "It's always been you too, you know that, right? I might've masked it, but it's always been you in my dreams."

"I know."

"You do?"

"Do you think I'd waste my life chasing you if I didn't?"

She kisses me gently and I hold my head to hers, deepening our kiss.

"You better be ready for me now that you caught me. You might want to throw me back one day."

I bring my lips to hers again, murmuring, "Not on your life."

EPILOGUE

Colton

One month later

I return home to find Juno sitting on the kitchen table in the same silk robe she wore that day her family came in and ruined her surprise for me. Her bag sits on one chair and her papers are piled in the corner of the table. Since Juno moved in a month ago, my house isn't as neat and orderly as it once was, but I don't care. All I care about is that she's with me every day.

"I thought we were picking our honeymoon destination tonight," I say.

She giggles. "We will later. Naked. In bed." She opens her legs and it's déjà vu all over again. "This is the redo I owe you."

Her ring sparkles in the light and I drop my bag, walking over and picking her up. "God, I love you."

She giggles until I ease her down on the floor by the fridge.

We're planning to get married next month. It was Juno's choice to have a winter wedding because she wanted to be my wife as soon as possible. I think she might be kissing my ass a little, but that's okay. As long as she's all right with being my wife and living with me, it's good enough for me.

"Cherry or strawberry?" I tease her lips with the fruit I pull out of the fridge.

"Colton, you have to strip."

"Oh shit, I forgot." I stand and toe out of my shoes, strip off my shirt, and get rid of my pants.

"Boxers too this time," she says.

I push them down my legs, getting naked for her while she takes the champagne and pours it down her front.

"Are we skipping over the eating part?" I ask her.

"You can eat me if you want." She falls onto her back.

She has to be kidding me—of course I want. But there's another part of the movie she's forgetting. I put my hand over the ice dispenser until an ice cube comes out. She looks up and says nothing, her back arching as though she wants it.

I melt it slightly in my mouth and bend over, trailing the ice cube over her stomach, around her nipples, and up her throat. She moans and squirms underneath me.

Picking up a cherry by the stem, I hang it in front of her mouth, and she bites it off the stem. Her hand travels down my chest, palming my hard length. This is what I've fantasized about all day—having her under me. When I trail what's left of the ice cube to her mound, her hand flies up behind her and hits the cupboard. A few of her business cards fall from the counter to the floor beside us.

"I forgot to ask, how was SparkFinder today?"

Juno's back at matchmaking, but most of her business meetings are held in town at Brewed Awakenings instead of in an actual office. Funny that she enjoys the pink mobile now since it lets her travel to the neighboring towns and hold events there or meet with clients who have called her.

"No business talk." She grabs my head and pulls me down to her. "It's not like I'm asking you how many pussies you're petting every day." I laugh, but she rolls me over, straddling me. "I think we were like this when we got interrupted."

She rocks back and forth, and without the friction of undergarments, the sensation makes my eyes roll back in my head. "Yeah, I think so too." I place my hands on her breasts. "I think my hands were here."

"If memory serves, yeah." She rises up and guides me into her. "And I think you were just like that." She moans.

"You might have been rocking," I remind her.

Then all jokes are put aside because we're both moaning our pleasure. Seeing that ring shining on her hand as she rides me takes me to the edge a lot faster these days. She rocks, digging her pelvis into mine as though she's looking for friction, so I take one hand and play with her clit as she rides me.

"I'm almost there. Don't stop." As if I would, she holds my wrist, riding me with wanton abandonment.

"Yoo hoo!" Dori's voice sounds out like the nightmare it is in this moment.

Juno stills then gets off me with wide eyes. "Didn't you lock the door?" she whisper-shouts.

I nod.

"I thought you got the key?"

"So did I."

We hide behind the island just like last time. Fucking hell.

"Again, you two?" Dori shakes her head. "Get in the car.

Kingston was in an accident at work. They assure me it's nothing serious, but we should go."

Juno tenses beside me and I ask, "You sure he's okay?"

"I'm telling you what they told me. I'm sure they wouldn't lie."

"Okay, let us get dressed. Grandma, you really have to start calling first," Juno says.

She shoos us with her hand. "I'm the reason you two are together, don't forget it."

And because she's kind of right, I keep my mouth shut and don't ask her for the key back—again.

MOST OF THE other Baileys are already in the waiting room when we arrive at the Anchorage hospital, since Dori waited for us to shower after I informed her that I could drive us. Apparently, that was her plan all along since Duke dropped her off at our place. I'll be happy when she's out of our business and on to another Bailey.

Juno beelines it over to pick up Easton, who adores her just as much as he adores his parents.

"Where's Phoenix?" Grandma Dori asks Griffin.

"She's coming. She's picking Sedona up at the airport," Griffin says.

"Sedona's coming home?" It's hard to surprise that woman but she looks genuinely shocked by the news.

Griffin shrugs.

"How long is she visiting for?" Savannah asks.

Griffin shrugs again.

Dori goes to the nurses' station and talks to someone, but they say it'll be awhile before Kingston can have visitors, since they're getting him settled.

"I don't get it, what happened?" I ask Austin.

"I guess he fell down a flight of stairs in the middle of the fire. But his chief just came over here and said he was fine when they brought him in. Maybe a concussion at worst. Doesn't seem to have broken anything."

I sit down next to him. "That's good, I guess." But I know Kingston's gonna be pissed if he's out of action for a while.

Trina, the nurse who helped me when Juno was here last month from the car accident, comes out of the back. Juno's too busy with Easton to notice, so I stand to talk to her.

"Do you remember me?"

She smiles. "I do. You're Kingston's friend."

"I am. Any chance we can see him?"

She looks over and cringes at the big family the big group. "Let me call back and see. Maybe half of you at a time?"

"Sure thing. Thanks."

She calls back then says the doctor says it's okay, that they're waiting on X-rays and MRI results.

"Half of us can go see him," I announce.

Everyone starts talking at the same time until finally it's decided that Dori, Juno, Savannah, and I will go first. We walk into the back, Juno's hand in mine. She might not say it, but I think being back here brings her back to when she thought she might lose me. Hell, seeing some of the other injuries from that accident made me happy hers weren't more serious.

Kingston seems surprised when we walk into the room. There're two nurses at his side, talking to him.

"Hey, guys," he says in a quiet voice.

The nurses each say goodbye with a wave, mentioning their shift is done.

We talk to him about what happened, and he says he's pretty sure he has a mild concussion, but they're going to run some more tests to be sure. As Juno and Dori talk to him, I try to get into Dori's purse to get my key back.

"Get out of my purse. Your key is always in a safe place." Dori pats her chest.

My mouth hangs open. She's got to be kidding me.

Then I hear someone come in the room behind us. "Hi, I'm the resident overseeing you today." She scribbles on the board then turns around. "How's the pain? Anything I can get you?"

Kingston's face loses all color. "Stella? Jesus, how hard did I hit my head?"

She steps back. "Kingston."

Juno looks at me and I nod, agreeing with her without her having to say a word. Let's get the hell out of here.

"Stella dear." Grandma Dori steps toward her and hugs her.

"Hi, Dori," she says, her eyes only on Kingston. "I'll be right back."

Kingston tries to get up, but cringes and his hand moves to his head.

Savannah pushes him back down on the bed by the shoulder. "You can't get up."

"But—"

"I'll go so someone else can come in." I dodge out of the room before an argument starts and walk down the hall.

In the waiting room, Austin stands and says he'll take my place.

"There's Phoenix and Sedona." Holly points down the hall, and everyone stands to greet them.

Before we get a chance to say our hellos, Sedona unbuttons her coat. "Let's just get this out of the way." She stands sideways, her hands running over her swollen belly.

My mouth drops open and silence fills the waiting room for a few weighted moments.

"You're pregnant?" Brooklyn screeches.

"No, she ate a watermelon," Phoenix says. "And she's moving back home."

Everyone looks at one another to gauge if anyone else knew, but it's clear that Phoenix and maybe Griffin are the only ones in the loop.

"Finally!" Harley screams and rushes over to Sedona. "I'm pregnant with someone." She bumps stomachs with her.

As if someone alerted them that there was a disturbance in the Bailey force, Savannah and Juno walk back into the waiting area and stop dead in their tracks.

"Does G'Ma D know?" Denver asks.

"No," Sedona says with a frown.

"She's about to," Rome says under his breath.

"Did you plan to reveal this in the hospital in case we actually kill her this time around?" Denver asks.

"No." Some of Sedona's earlier bravado vanishes.

"Well, I'm just saying kudos if you did because she's dealt with a lot from us, but this." He twirls his finger at her belly and shakes his head.

"Next time she wants your opinion, I'll remind her she doesn't," Phoenix says to him, putting her arm around Sedona as if she's a wounded bird.

Huh. There must be a lot more we don't know yet.

"A child is a blessing," Harley says. "No matter the circumstances."

As if she knows the tension needs to be broken, Calista walks up to Denver. "Uncle Denver, let's play thumb wars."

"Sure thing, little one." He puts his hand in hers, and a moment later, he looks at Sedona. "I'm sorry. You know we have your back and that baby is lucky to have you as a mom." He leans closer. "But should I book a flight to New York?"

A tear slips from Sedona's eye.

"I'll take that as a yes," he says, looking at all the men in the group as though they're paying Jamison a visit.

"Just to keep everyone in the loop, Stella is back too." Savannah takes Brinley from Liam, rocking her on her hip.

They all look at one another as though they're bracing themselves for hurricane Bailey that's about to make landfall.

The End

COCKAMAMIE UNICORN RAMBLINGS

We have a confession, neither one of are huge fans of the friends-to-lovers storyline. Which is probably why you don't see a lot of them from us. But Juno and Colton were a little different for us. We've spent so much time with the Baileys that we were rooting for them to find their HEA and excited to write this book! We had to dig deep to know why they never found their way to one another and if they had (which now you know they had) what continued to keep them apart.

We're going to share a secret with you. Juno was going to be pregnant and it was going to have happened the night of the baby shower. We planned that out back while writing Confessions but then when it came time to write the story-line, and we had made him engaged at the end of the book, we didn't think Colton is the type of guy to cheat no matter how long he's loved Juno or how fake his engagement was. And we didn't think that spoke to Juno either. So, then we were going to make her pregnant later in the book, but it all just seemed wrong. We scraped the entire thing. BUT she was *never* the unknown female in Operation Bailey Babies. I guess now you know who was. ;)

We opted for the a less angsty storyline because we felt it was realistic for the characters we created and you've read about since the beginning of the series—real life best friends who turned into lovers after years of resisting fate. Either the timing was wrong, or they're dating other people at different times, or they're just petrified of losing that other person in their life if things go south. But in the end love made it impossible for them to be apart!

SUPER HUGE THANKS to our team who if not for them, we'd never be able to finish these books!

Danielle Sanchez and the entire Wildfire Marketing Solutions!

Cassie from Joy Editing for line edits.

Ellie from My Brother's Editor for line edits.

Shawna from Behind the Writer for proofreading.

Sarah from Okay Creations for the cover and branding for the entire series.

Sara from Sara Eirew Photography for the super sexy picture of Juno and Colton.

Bloggers who consistently carve out time to read, review and/or promote us.

Our Piper Rayne Unicorns who champion this series to others with their whole hearts.

You the reader who took a chance on our book with so many choices out there.

You finally met Stella! What did you think? Is she what you expected? Just like Juno and Colton, there's a lot you don't know about Kingston and Stella's story. We have some twists coming. Ones we thought of while writing Secrets of the World's Worst Matchmaker and we can't wait for you to read their story. Who doesn't love a hero who knows what he wants? And Kingston wants Stella whether he admits it to her or not.

XO,
    Piper & Rayne

ABOUT PIPER & RAYNE

Piper Rayne is a USA Today Bestselling Author duo who write "heartwarming humor with a side of sizzle" about families, whether that be blood or found. They both have e-readers full of one-clickable books, they're married to husbands who drive them to drink, and they're both chauffeurs to their kids. Most of all, they love hot heroes and quirky heroines who make them laugh, and they hope you do, too!

My Famous Frenemy

The Greene Family Vacation

My Scorned Best Friend

My Fake Fiancé

My Brother's Forbidden Friend

The Modern Love World

Charmed by the Bartender

Hooked by the Boxer

Mad about the Banker

Complete Set (all 3 books)

The Single Dad's Club

Real Deal

Dirty Talker

Sexy Beast

Complete Set (all 3 books)

Hollywood Hearts

Mister Mom

Animal Attraction

Domestic Bliss

Bedroom Games

Cold as Ice

On Thin Ice

Break the Ice

Complete Set (all 3 books +)

Charity Case

Manic Monday

Afternoon Delight

Happy Hour

Complete Set (all 3 books)

Blue Collar Brothers

Flirting with Fire

Crushing on the Cop

Engaged to the EMT

Complete Set (All 3 books)

White Collar Brothers

Sexy Filthy Boss

Dirty Flirty Enemy

Wild Steamy Hook-up

The Rooftop Crew

My Bestie's Ex

A Royal Mistake

The Rival Roomies

Our Star-Crossed Kiss

The Do-Over

A Co-Workers Crush

Hockey Hotties

Countdown to a Kiss (Free Novella)

My Lucky #13

The Trouble with #9

Faking it with #41

Sneaking around with #34

Second Shot with #76

Offside with #55